BEASTS —OF— OLYMPUS

by Lucy Coats   art by Brett Bean

THE HEROIC COLLECTION

PENGUIN WORKSHOP
An Imprint of Penguin Random House

PENGUIN WORKSHOP
Penguin Young Readers Group
An Imprint of Penguin Random House LLC

Text copyright © 2015 by Lucy Coats. Illustrations copyright © 2015 by Brett Bean. All rights reserved. *Beast Keeper, Hound of Hades,* and *Steeds of the Gods* first published in 2015 by Grosset & Dunlap. This bind-up edition published in 2018 by Penguin Workshop, an imprint of Penguin Random House LLC, 345 Hudson Street, New York, New York 10014. PENGUIN and PENGUIN WORKSHOP are trademarks of Penguin Books Ltd, and the W colophon is a trademark of Penguin Random House LLC. Printed in the USA.

The Library of Congress has cataloged the individual books under the following Control Numbers: *Beast Keeper:* 2014041137, *Hound of Hades:* 2014041139, *Steeds of the Gods:* 2015006964

ISBN 9781524790646   10 9 8 7 6 5 4 3 2 1

TABLE OF CONTENTS

For Findlay, Lochlan, and Paloma,
from their Grande-Tante Ancienne

BEASTS
—OF—
OLYMPUS

by Lucy Coats   art by Brett Bean

Beast Keeper

CHAPTER 1

THE GOD FATHER

Demon was chatting to the chickens about eggs when his dad arrived. He'd never met his dad before, but he knew it was him all right. His dad had:

Thick, hairy, goaty legs.

Big curly horns.

Yellow eyes with black, slitted pupils.

No clothes to speak of.

And a set of silver reed pipes.

Demon's dad was a god.

"Foxgodfoxgodfoxgodrunrunrunsquaww-wwkkkk!" The chickens scattered across the yard, gabbling and squawking in terror. Demon kneeled in the dirt and bowed his head. He wasn't too sure if that's what you did with a dad, but it was certainly what you did with a god. Especially if that god was Pan, ruler of forests and all wild creatures. A god who could call up a pack of hungry bears that could rip you to bits in an instant.

"Pandemonius, my boy!" said his dad. Pan's voice was like mossy bark on ancient trees. It was deep and velvety with a hint of crumbly roughness at the edges.

Even though it was Demon's real name, no one ever called him Pandemonius. Even the mountain wolves called him Demon—and they tended to be rather formal in their speech. Demon was about to tell his dad how silly his full name sounded, when he felt a pair of huge hands under his armpits. He was lifted up into a god hug that smelled of pungent green things like goaty musk and old, stale blood.

"Good to meet you at last, my son. C'mon, let's find your dear mother, Carys, and get your things together. Haven't seen her in far too long. Not since you arrived in the world, in fact. By Zeus's beard, how time flies."

About two minutes later, a confused Demon found himself in the corner of the hut he shared with his mother. As he packed his few possessions into a bundle, he could see his dad whispering in his mom's ear. When she'd seen Demon and his father walk in together, she dropped her best herb-chopping knife on the hard dirt floor. It nearly cut off her big toe. Now she kept saying, "But, but, but," in a high-pitched voice. She sounded like Demon's little black lamb, Barley, did when he wanted milk. She might as well have kept quiet. Pan stomped over her *buts* like a charging centaur.

"Pandemonius is coming with me," he said at last. "And that's final. You don't want to offend the gods by refusing to let him go, now, do you?"

There was nothing much his mom could say to that, really. Mortals who offended gods usually ended up as little piles of scorched ash, or trees, or rocks. In the end, Pan dragged Demon forcibly out the door without more than a quick good-bye kiss and hug. A weeping Carys was left behind them waving a damp hankie.

Demon felt like crying, too. His mom was his whole family. He felt a fat, bumpy lump swelling bigger and bigger in his throat until he nearly couldn't breathe. He didn't dare ask where he was being taken, or what for. Even if he had dared, he didn't know what to call his father, anyway. Your Godness? Your Holiness? Your Dadness? Until a few minutes ago, he'd been an ordinary eleven-year-old boy, living with his mom near an ordinary village in the middle of Arcadia. He spent his days looking after the goats and sheep and chickens, and hoeing the vegetables.

Although the fact that he could talk to animals *was* out of the ordinary. Everyone around his home knew he was the child of a god, and things like that happened to half-god kids. No one took much notice, really, except for the local farmers calling him in when their beasts were sick. Demon could find out what was wrong so his mom could say what herbs to prescribe for them. All the farmers got used to hearing Demon tell them that a sheep was saying, "My belly hurts," instead of just "Baaaaah." Now he was being wrenched away from everything he knew, all in an instant, by a father he didn't even know how to speak to.

When they got to the edge of the forest, Pan stopped.

"IRIS!" The god bellowed. "EXPRESS FOR TWO! OLYMPUS BOUND!"

Demon felt his fat, bumpy throat lump get bigger still. Olympus? Why was he being taken to Olympus? That was where all the gods lived. What were they going to do to him? A horrid thought hit his brain like a speeding arrow. He couldn't remember if the gods still liked human sacrifices or not. Perhaps that was what he was wanted for. Only . . . why had he packed all his stuff if they were just going to kill him? It wasn't like Zeus was going to want his spare cloak, was it? Just then, right in front of his eyes, a rainbow burst from the sky and landed at their feet.

"Hop on, son," said Pan. "Hold tight to me. The Iris Express can go a bit fast if you're not used to it."

Demon did as he was told. He squeezed his eyes shut and hung on to Pan's big hairy waist. He felt his stomach drop away behind him. There was a loud whooshing sound and a strong smell of flowers. *Wild roses*, he thought, sniffing cautiously. He opened one eye a crack and looked down. Then he wished he hadn't. He was standing on a see-through wisp of rainbow that was whizzing up in an arch into the sky. The earth was getting smaller and smaller behind him. The whole of Greece was laid out below like a wiggly green-and-amber hand in a dark purple pool of sea. He was just about to scream with terror when there was another whoosh and a thump. They burst through a misty barrier and landed.

"Here we are," said Pan. He strode down off the rainbow toward some shining white temples.

Everything was enormous and very clean on Olympus (though Demon could smell an odd and rather nasty sort of pooey stench in the air). There were all kinds of nymphs and cherubs flitting about among gigantic multicolored blooms and trees with bunches of silvery golden fruit hanging from them. Demon had to run to keep up with Pan. His bundle banged against his back. Suddenly, he felt really angry. How dare his dad just turn up and kidnap him like this without telling him anything? It wasn't *fair*! If he was going to be sizzled and frizzled as a sacrifice, he wanted to know why.

"Hey!" Demon yelled. "Hey, you! Stop!"

Pan stopped. He turned around very slowly, his eyes flashing green fire. The nymphs and cherubs flicked out of sight rather abruptly.

"Are you yelling 'Hey, you!' at ME, boy?" he asked, very quietly.

Demon gulped a bit, but he wasn't going to back down. He nodded. His mom always said his worst fault was that he never knew when to be polite and keep his mouth shut in front of his elders and betters, but this time he just didn't care.

"Yes . . . um, sir—Your Godness-Pan-Dad. I w-want to know w-what you're g-going to d-do to me." Demon didn't want his voice to stammer and stumble, but it seemed to have a mind of its own. He cleared his throat and tried again. "If I'm going to be a sacrifice to the gods, I think you should have let me say good-bye to Mom properly first. She's going to be really upset with you when I'm dead."

Pan looked at him. The green eye fire died, and his mouth opened in a great windy gust of laughter that nearly knocked Demon backward.

"Sacrifice to the gods? Is that what you thought you were here for? My own son? Did you hear that, nymphs, a SACRIFICE? That's a good one!" He laughed some more, and the nymphs and cherubs flicked into view again, looking relieved. Pan scratched at a curly horn and ran a hand through his wild hair. Bits of bark, twig, and dead leaf fell out in showers. "By Zeus's toenails! I told your dear mom, but I forgot I hadn't told you. C'mon, boy, follow me, quick as you can. I think it's high time I took you to see the Stables of the Gods."

CHAPTER 2

THE STABLES OF THE GODS

The Stables of the Gods were extremely smelly.
There was no getting around it. The long, tall
building stank like a mixture of centuries-old
dead fish and a thousand years of ancient poo.
There was a roaring rumpus of beasts and
monsters in every pen and stable. The noise
was indescribably loud. Pan backed out of the
Stables and put his hands over his hairy ears.
He beckoned Demon over to a bench under a
tree a little way away, where it was a bit quieter.

He still had to shout, though.

"All the gods and goddesses are complaining about the stink getting into their clothes—and the racket is spoiling everyone's sleep. Old Silenus the satyr looked after the beasts for ages, but then he annoyed Hera one time too many. So she got Zeus to banish him down to earth. A place called Lydia, I think, near some king's palace. Dionysus got him out of trouble there, too . . . Anyway, then I had one of my fauns look after the Stables, but he got bitten by a basilisk. Since then it's all gone to Hades a bit." He cleared his throat. "Zeus asked me to find someone who was good with animals. I thought you might like to have a go at the job. You've done pretty well with mortal beasts, and immortal creatures aren't so very different— barring a fang or two."

Demon opened his mouth, then shut it again.

He didn't know what to say. But he felt quite relieved that he wasn't going to be a sacrifice.

Pan went on. "Zeus and the others are prepared to give you a trial run as a stable boy to see if you're any good at it—and we'll set you up with a magical healing thingamajig so you don't get killed in the first five minutes. If you're a success, you'll get an official title and some proper pay. What do you say, boy? Will you give it a go?" Demon looked at his dad. There was bound to be a catch—there always was with gods. His mom had drummed that into him since he was tiny.

"Do I get a choice?" he asked.

Pan looked at him and smiled widely. His teeth were square and yellow and flecked with green and red. "I know how much you love animals, and how they love you back. Of course you have a choice." He paused here and smiled a little wider—a dangerous smile this time. "But on the other hand, if you offend all the Olympians by refusing even to give it a try . . ."

He didn't have to say any more than that. Demon knew he was stuck with the job for now, whether he wanted it or not. And it was true what his dad had said—he did love animals. Perhaps it would be okay. It might even be exciting. "What do I have to do?" he asked.

"Hephaestus will fill you in," said Pan. "He's the smith god, you know. Clever fellow with his hands. He makes all sorts of marvelous thingies for us. I'll take you to meet him now. Maybe if you ask nicely, he'll lend you one of his metal men to help with the clean-up." He sniffed, his large nostrils flaring like a hound on a scent. "Don't take too long to get rid of the smell, or the goddesses are bound to come after you. Best not tempt them."

On this comforting thought, he turned and walked away. Demon followed him, trying hard not to think of angry goddesses.

———————◆———————

Hephaestus turned out to live inside a mountain. He was hammering at his forge when Pan and Demon walked in.

"Just a minute," he yelled. "Got to finish this sword for Ares. He's always breaking them in one of his idiotic wars. The crazy fool."

Demon watched with amazement.

Hephaestus grabbed the blazing metal with his bare hands, as a creature that seemed to be made of gold and silver pumped the bellows.

"One of my automaton robots," shouted Hephaestus when he saw Demon looking at the metal creature. "I made it a while ago to help in the forge. Not much for chatting, but it's great at keeping the heat steady. I've got lots of different kinds. Useful creatures, these robots."

There was a final clang, and the smith god put down his tools.

"Ah," he continued. "Young Pandemonius, is it? We've all heard about you and the wonders you're going to perform in the Stables. Your dad's been singing your praises, you know. Very proud of you. Chip off the old block, eh?"

Pan cleared his throat and looked embarrassed (if a god could look embarrassed).

"I've got to go now," Demon's father said. "There's trouble with my satyrs in Caria—always fighting, those boys. Look after my son, Heffy. Don't want him eaten! Now, Pandemonius. You do what Hephaestus tells you. He'll sort you out. Give you what you need to get started, that sort of thing. I'll come and see you again when I can."

Pan fumbled in what seemed to be a pocket in his hairy thigh, pulled out a battered set of reed pipes, and handed them to Demon. "My spare set. Good for calming awkward beasts. Just tootle away and they should settle down. Be careful," he said. "It doesn't always work on all of them, so you take care." He patted Demon on the head, nearly knocking him over, and turned away.

Demon felt the bumpy throat lump come back. He hadn't known his dad was proud of him, or that Pan had been watching over him. It made him go a bit warm and fuzzy inside, but now he just hoped he wasn't going to mess it all up. Immortal beasts were going to be very different from chickens and goats, whatever his dad thought.

"Now," said Hephaestus in a voice that was meant to be reassuring but somehow wasn't, "sit on this barrel here and have a cup of ambrosia. Then we'll go and get you settled in." He handed

Demon a goblet full of golden liquid that smelled wonderful. Unfortunately it didn't taste quite as good as it smelled, and Demon spat it out at once.

"Ugh!" he said, spluttering. "What's *that*? It's really disgusting."

"That's the food of the gods," Hephaestus said. "Ambrosia, we call it—comes in both liquid and cake form. You might like the cake more. You'd better get used to it, boy, because it's all there is up here unless it's a feast day. Anyway, it's good for you. Makes you stronger than normal mortals. Gives you muscles like a hero. Ah, that reminds me. Better give you one of my healing charms, or your puny mortal body won't last any time at all in the Stables."

He walked over to a shelf and took down a thin bronze collar shaped like two coiled snakes biting their own tails. The snakes had ruby eyes and seemed to writhe as Demon looked at them.

"Put this around your neck. The snakes are
called Offy and Yukus. They'll sort out pretty
much anything in the way of bites or stings
or anything some of those vicious creatures
will throw at you. Just try not to get your head
chomped off. That'll be almost impossible
for them to mend. Now, let's go and get you
introduced to the Stables properly."

CHAPTER 3

THE BEASTLY BEASTS

As Demon curled up in a pile of straw that night, he knew he had never been more exhausted. Hephaestus had pointed out which creature was which and shown him where the brooms and buckets and pitchforks and wheelbarrows were. He explained how to get to the muckheap and how to use the magic chute that sent all the poo down to feed the hundred-armed monsters in Tartarus, and then left him to it.

"There's a loft above the unicorns. You can

sleep there," Hephaestus had said. "I think the faun left his blanket. The nymphs come around with fresh ambrosia cakes for you and leftovers for the beasts twice a day—and you can get water from the naiad's spring outside. Remember to thank Melanie the naiad, though, or she'll cover you in waterweed. If you have any problems, come and find me." He'd waved a casual hand and walked out, leaving Demon all alone in the midst of the noise and chaos—and the smell.

Demon had put his bundle down and just stood there. "Talk about being thrown in the deep end," he muttered resentfully. There was just so much to take in and sort out. He'd never seen so many different beasts—most of them dangerous, magical, and with hard-to-remember names. He needed to think. "SHUT UP!" he bawled. To his surprise, it worked. Kind of. The noise fell by at least a quarter. "Thank you. Now let's sort this mess out. Who's the smelliest? I'm going to start with them." Immediately the noise rose to a higher pitch than ever. But Demon could hear two words being repeated over and over in lots of strange and different voices.

"STINKY COWS! STINKY COWS! STINKY COWS!"

He looked down the Stables and saw a huge pen of rather shamefaced horned heads hanging over the rails. They were the famous Cattle of the Sun, resting after months of being dragged back from the lands of Geryon, the giant slain by the famous hero Heracles.

"We can't help it," they mooed. "It's that leftover ambrosia cake. It doesn't suit any of our stomachs. It gives us terrible gas!"

The other beasts jeered and hissed as Demon walked toward them and tried to avoid the row of snapping jaws and tearing claws on either side.

"STINKY COWS! STINKY COWS! STINKY COWS!"

It was sadly true. The Cattle of the Sun stank more than any of the other beasts. They reeked. No wonder the whole of Olympus smelled of poo. Demon staggered back from their pen and bumped into the barred door of a stable opposite. A large clawed paw lashed out and caught him on the shoulder, ripping his tunic and tearing deep into his flesh. It hurt so much that Demon jerked away and fell to his knees, trying not to scream. Immediately the snakes on his collar whipped around and plunged their tongues into the wound. It stopped hurting at once, and he could feel the gash closing up.

"Th-th-thanks," he whispered. Offy and Yukus coiled themselves back around his neck.

"It wasssss our pleasssssure," they hissed into his ear.

Demon got up slowly and turned around. A huge creature with the head and wings of an eagle and a lion's body stared at him with golden eyes. Demon walked forward and put his hands on the bars. It was important not to show he was afraid. Animals didn't respect you if you were frightened.

"You're a griffin, aren't you?" he asked. The creature spat, and the spit sizzled slightly as it hit the ground.

"Yes," it said aggressively. "So?" Its sharp beak darted out and clacked shut just by his ear. Demon dodged away just in time to avoid another serious injury.

"So, I'm here to look after you all," Demon said in a loud, firm voice (even though he was quaking like a pile of jellied eels inside). "Zeus's orders. If you want clean beds and someone to listen to what you need, then you'll quit the clawing and biting stuff." His voice dropped, and became what he hoped was threatening. "I'm quite sure Zeus would be VERY interested to hear that you were trying to kill the stable boy HE appointed. He wouldn't be very pleased. In fact he might even come and PAY YOU A VISIT." Demon held his breath and waited. Surely no one wanted a visit from Zeus.

But the griffin wasn't backing down. It spat at him again, hitting the hem of his tunic, and making a big smoking hole. "Hate humans," it hissed.

Demon crouched down in front of it. "Why do you hate humans?" he asked. The griffin snorted.

"We ALL hate humans," it snarled. "Specially half-god humans like you. That's what most of the heroes are, see? The gods send us down to the earthly realms to fight them or give them some sort of adventure. We're immortal, of course, so we can't really die. After we get 'killed' down there, we come back up here to recover. And then they send us back down to do it all over again. No one really cares about us beasts. We're just entertainment—a bit of fun for the gods—their dangerous little pets." Then a whole chorus of angry voices joined in.

Yes. A bit of fun.

You should see my spear scars.

That Heracles is the worst. Always off destroying us beasts.

I got a lump of burning lead shoved down my throat.

I got my tails chopped off.

I have to spend every day tearing out some poor guy's liver—and I don't even like liver.
IT'S NOT FAIR!

As the noise grew louder and louder, Demon remembered his dad's pipes. He got them out and blew a long series of silvery notes. Immediate silence. It was like a miracle.

"You poor things," he said into the quiet. "That all sounds terrible. But look at me! I'm not a hero. I may be the son of Pan, but really I'm just a scrawny boy who loves all creatures, tame or wild. And I'd never hurt any of you." He paused. "I-I'm all alone up here s-so I'd really like us to be friends. I promise to do my best for you. Will you help me?" One of the tears he'd been holding back for so long escaped and trickled down his cheek. He brushed it away crossly as the griffin glared down its beak at him, poked out a very long forked tongue, and licked its beak meaningfully.

"You threatened us with a visit from Zeus, Pan's scrawny kid. I don't like threats. How about the rest of you?" Any normal human would just have heard a cacophony of growls and moos and squeaks and snarls and roars and barks and howls.

Demon just heard:

"NO."

CHAPTER 4

THE STABLE BOY

Demon was exhausted every single night from
then on. He just curled up in his bed of straw,
pulled the faun's spider-silk blanket over him,
and slept like a dead person. He was bitten
and bruised and clawed and stung at least
twenty times a day by various beasts. Offy and
Yukus had to work on him pretty much full
time to keep him alive. Hephaestus had lent
him one of his metal robots for a few days, and
together they had shoveled and forked and

wheelbarrowed what seemed like enough beast poo to create several new muckheap mountains. Demon thought he could hear the hundred-armed monsters roaring their appreciation at their massive poo feast from the bottom of the chute.

Demon had talked to Hephaestus about the Cattle of the Sun and their windy stomachs. Thankfully the smith god had asked Helios, the sun god, for some of the special golden hay he fed his horses. That had solved the problem, and now the cattle sparkled and shone and—more to the point—smelled of nothing but the aroma of clean, well-fed beasts. There was no chance of the gods or goddesses complaining now, he hoped.

He didn't have much to do with the gods really, apart from Hephaestus, who was turning out to be quite kind, for an immortal. There was just the occasional flash, whoosh, and thump as the Iris Express landed, or a brief message via a cherub requesting that this beast or that be made ready to go down to the earthly realms, or the crack and roar of thunder and lightning from Zeus and Hera's big palace on the farthest hill. Demon didn't mind—the less he had to do with the gods, the better, he thought.

Outside his work at the Stables, Demon was almost happy. He missed his mom a lot, of course, but the nymphs and naiads and dryads soon began to treat him like a little brother. They teased him and told him snippets of gossip about the gods and goddesses. In this way he learned that Zeus was a terrible flirt who was always getting into trouble with his wife, that Dionysus had invented a new kind of grape drink that made everybody very giggly and silly, that Aphrodite had just redecorated her palace in fifty different shades of pink and was always meddling in the lives of mortal lovers . . . and that Hera was best avoided at all times, if you knew what was good for you.

Inside the Stables he was learning to deal with his charges little by little. They saw that he really did seem to care about their welfare, and most of them tolerated him. Even the griffin was becoming friendlier. It only bit him halfheartedly now, and Demon suspected it might even have a sense of humor when he found out that it liked to hide in a dark corner of its cage and then leap out at him. It was certainly becoming much chattier, and it seemed to enjoy giving him advice. The job he liked best was exercising the little herd of Ethiopian winged horses. He brushed and brushed them until their coats shone like ivory and onyx and bronze. Then he polished their little gold horns and wiped their wings down with scented oil he found in the storeroom. The boss horse was called Keith, and at first he had tended to snap and bite and rear when Demon tried to get on his back. However, after Demon had discovered that he liked his left ear scratched in a certain way, they'd come to an arrangement. Ten minutes scratching equaled a half-hour exercise flight. Demon thought that was *very* fair. So every day he found himself soaring through the air over Olympus at the head of six flying horses. They flew a loop-the-loop over Hephaestus's mountain and chased the fiery spark spirits high into the atmosphere. It was definitely better than herding goats and sheep, he reckoned.

Not all the beasts were as easy to please as Keith, though. It had taken him a whole week to learn how to get near enough to feed the unicorns, let alone milk them. There'd been a series of increasingly angry messages from Aphrodite (who wanted her annual unicorn milk bath), and so he'd had to ask for advice fast.

"How do you milk a unicorn, please?" he politely asked Melanie the water naiad as he filled the buckets at her spring. But she was busy admiring her new necklace of raindrops and wouldn't answer him. The cherubs just giggled and pelted him with petals. The nymphs were more helpful.

"They like girls," said the head nymph, whose name was Althea.

Demon looked at her. "Don't know if you'd noticed," he said, slightly sarcastically, "but I'm not one."

That started a lot of giggling and nudging, but Althea just looked at her sisters and they fell silent.

"We owe you," she said. "Those smelly Stables were just about killing our noses—we all felt really sick until you came along and cleaned up. So one of us will do the milking for you morning and evening, if you'll let us have the wool from the Golden Ram when you shear him. It makes the finest embroidery thread, you know, and we like it for decorating our dresses."

"It's a deal," said Demon. He had never sheared a winged sheep before, but was willing to try anything to get Aphrodite off his back.

CHAPTER 5

THE HOSPITAL SHED

Demon felt that he'd really settled into his new job, when the casualties started coming in to the Stables. The Nemean Lion was first. He arrived one morning on the Iris Express, and immediately an alarm in the Stables started to sound.

"Incoming wounded, incoming wounded," squawked a carved head on the back wall. Demon had wondered what it was for, and now he knew. He started to panic at once.

"What do I do?" he asked the griffin, whose clawed toenails he was clipping at the time. The griffin nodded toward a long, low wagon that stood propped against the end wall of the Stables.

"Off you go with that," he said. "Iris usually dumps the wounded at the foot of the Express for someone to collect and bring back. Whoever is hurt needs to go in the hospital shed to be patched up. You do know where that is, don't you?"

Demon shook his head. How could he have been so stupid? On his very first day, the beasts had told him they often got hurt. Why hadn't he checked the hospital out? He shot out of the griffin's stable, forgetting to latch the door behind him. He grabbed the stretcher wagon and started to run, cursing himself all the way. He'd helped out plenty of normal animals with his mom, but he didn't have her healing herbs or bandages or anything here—and he absolutely hated seeing an animal in pain.

What he found at the foot of the Iris Express was worse than he could ever have imagined. A huge, bald pink lion lay there, moaning in agony.

"My skin, my special skin," it groaned.

Demon approached cautiously. Its skin might have gone, but its claws and teeth were definitely still present.

"I'm Demon," he said softly, squatting down beside it. "Will you let me help you?"

The lion rolled its eyes and groaned some more as Demon hauled it onto the stretcher as gently as he could. It bit him twice, and scratched him seventeen times, but the magic snakes whipped into action, and the blood stopped oozing in almost no time at all. Demon hardly noticed—he was too busy trying to work out what he should do with the poor thing.

"Over here," yelled the griffin. It flicked its door open with a paw and escaped from its open cage. "Lucky for you I'm not the Minotaur, or you might have been in big trouble, Pan's scrawny kid," it said.

The griffin pointed a claw at a big thatched shed right at the back of the Stables. Demon had thought it was a storage shed of some kind. Sorting out the main Stables had taken all his time and energy, so he hadn't checked it out yet.

Then the griffin saw the Nemean Lion and whistled through its beak. "By Chiron's hooves, mate. Who got *you*? That's a terrible state you're in."

"Heracles," moaned the lion. "Hera's set him twelve impossible tasks as a punishment for killing his poor wife and children. Apparently she's got a little list marked 'Labors for Heracles,' and she's going to tick them off one by one." The lion moaned some more. "He's gone and ripped off my poor skin and made it into invincible armor. Heracles was bad enough before, but now none of us are safe. I'm only the first casualty you'll have to deal with, you mark my words."

With that, its eyes rolled up in its skinless head, and it fainted. Demon looked around the shelves. There were dirty, unrolled bandages, half-empty bottles, spilled herbs, and a variety of blunt instruments that looked as if they'd been used for cutlery.

"Silenus wasn't great at doctoring," said the griffin, stating the obvious. Demon stared at the lion in despair. He hadn't a clue where to start mending it. The griffin came over and head-butted him gently. "I'd have a word with Hephaestus," it advised him. "He's a god who cares enough to fix most things. Unlike most of the others," it muttered bitterly.

By the time he reached Hephaestus's mountain, Demon was panting like a boy who'd run four marathons. He had to drink a whole glass of the revolting ambrosia before he could even speak. When he'd explained the problem, Hephaestus scratched his head.

"You need some of my magic bandages, I should think," he said. "I keep them around in case any of the nymphs come in here and get burned. Happens sometimes when the forge is at full blast and I don't notice them standing there. Should help soothe the lion down—and then we can think about making him a new pelt. You can get the Caucasian Eagle to nip over to Pandora's house on his way back from tearing old Prometheus's liver out, and ask Epimetheus if he has any skin left over from making all those furry earth animals."

Hephaestus rummaged around on the shelves to the left of the furnace and pulled out a square green package that smelled of the familiar scent of lavender and aloe, with something Demon didn't recognize thrown in. "Here you are—slap that all over him for now. I'll be along in a bit to see how you're doing."

The lion did look funny covered in sticky green gauze, but he also seemed to be more comfortable. Demon fed him leftover ambrosia through a straw when he woke, and then the lion told him about the fight with Heracles. By the time he'd finished, Demon reckoned that if he ever met Heracles, he was going to punch the wretched hero on the nose . . . however strong and big he was. Nice people did NOT go around pulling skins off poor innocent lions.

Later that night, Hephaestus turned up as promised. He limped into the hospital shed carrying a large silver box with brass handles, which he set down on the floor.

"Should have given you this before, really," he said. "It's got the same sort of magic in it as Offy and Yukus use on you—only it's for beasts. Just open it when you've got a medical emergency, and you'll find it tells you what you need for most cases. Think it'll provide a cure for just about anything that happens to your beasts. There's this, too." He handed over a short length of silver rope. "Ties anything. Expands as needed. Won't come undone. And I ground some of my calming crystals into the core of it in case your dad's pipes aren't handy. You can belt it around your tunic."

Demon forgot Hephaestus was one of the gods. He jumped up and hugged him.

"Thanks, Heffy," he said. "You're the best!" Hephaestus grinned down at him and ruffled his hair.

"Irreverent cub," he said. "Don't you go calling Zeus 'Zeusie,' now, or you'll find yourself a pile of ash faster than you can blink. And mind you don't forget to send that message with the Caucasian Eagle. You definitely need new skin for the lion—but unfortunately the box won't provide enough of it. It only does patches."

When the Caucasian Eagle returned the next day, it was carrying a small bag in its claws. "Here you are," it said, dropping it at Demon's feet. "Epimetheus says that's the very last of the skin, so don't go asking for any more. Now, where's my ambrosia? Filthy stuff, but it takes away the taste of liver. I REALLY hate that wretched liver," it grumbled, flying off to its perch and tucking its head under its wing.

Demon thanked it and picked up the bag, yawning. He'd been up with the Nemean Lion all night, playing Pan's pipes to soothe it, changing its dressings in between scrubbing and tidying up the hospital shed.

"Let's have a look," he said, upending the bag on the now shiny, clean counter. There was a tiny but distinct silence as he and the lion looked at what had fallen out. There was no getting away from it. The skin that Epimetheus had sent was spotty with a hint of fluff. It was also a strange shade of bright green. "Er, perhaps it's just gone a bit moldy and it'll wash off," Demon said in an optimistic tone. He wasn't hopeful, though. When he brushed at the skin, it stayed firmly green. Like new grass.

"I'll be a laughingstock," moaned the lion. "Lions have flat, tawny skin. If you put that on me, I'll be the Greater Green-Spotted Nemean Lion."

"Think of it as a fashion statement," said Demon encouragingly. "I'm sure all the lady lions will love it. Would you rather stay as you are and be the Lesser Pink Bald Nemean Lion?"

"Go on, then," said the lion. "I don't care anymore. I shall ask the gods to let me go into retirement in a nice lonely cave somewhere, if they insist on sending me back to the earthly realms."

The new skin fit—just. It was a bit of a tight squeeze, and there were a couple of odd bulgy lumps where Demon had had to smooth and squash bits of lion into rather too little skin—but at least the Nemean Lion looked like a lion again (though a very oddly colored and slightly fluffy one).

Demon put him into a nice darkened stable to rest—and Hephaestus brought over some meaty scraps from one of the god feasts. The lion gobbled them up in seconds. Demon's first medical emergency seemed to be over, and he hadn't even needed to use the silver box. He felt quite proud of himself.

CHAPTER 6

THE BRONZE BIRDS

All was quiet for a week or so. The Nemean Lion was getting used to its strange skin and had recovered enough to begin some playful chasing of Artemis's five golden-horned deer (though it promised Demon it wouldn't hurt them). Once the rest of the beasts in the Stables had seen what Demon had done for the Nemean Lion, they accepted the animal totally—with the exception of the giant scorpion.

Then the carved head began to squawk

again. "Incoming wounded. Incoming wounded. Lots of incoming wounded," it shouted.

Demon rushed for the wagon. This time he remembered to lock the cage door behind him. No one would have been happy if the giant scorpion had escaped. It hated everybody and liked nothing better than stabbing its huge stinger into the gentler beasts and dangling them up in the air over its pincers. Demon didn't trust it an inch after he'd found that out for himself, and now he usually approached the scary creature with a long, pointy fending-off stick when he fed it.

When he got to the Iris Express, there was a whole flock of large, almost featherless birds scattered all over the ground. "Heracles?" he asked. The birds nodded and clacked their beaks. What remained of their feathers rattled as he lifted each one carefully onto his mobile stretcher.

"Careful," said one. "Don't cut yourself."

When Demon looked more closely, he noticed that the feathers were made of pure, shiny bronze. He also noticed that all the birds had razor-sharp teeth inside their beaks.

"You're the Stymphalian Birds, aren't you?" he asked as he trundled them into the hospital shed. "Do you want to tell me what happened?"

"We were just finishing off this tasty maiden we'd found washing some horrid dirty clothes in our nice clean lake—very juicy and tender she was, too—when there was this horrible noise," squawked the bird who had spoken before. It seemed to be the leader of the flock. "Sort of a rattly racket that got into our ears and made us fly up in the air. Next thing we knew, there were arrows coming at us from the other side of the water. We saw that horrible hero Heracles, with that huge bow of his, shooting away at us. Poor

Boneyfeet over there copped an arrow right in the head—blood everywhere. Very nasty—we nearly had to leave him behind for the fishes to nibble.

"Well, we fired our bronze feathers right back at him, same as we always do—only he wouldn't stop. We called up to Ares when we realized we were going to be in trouble if we carried on firing—and he sent the Iris Express down for us." The bird looked at Demon with a bright orange eye. "Can you fix us up? Ares says there's a nice island we can go to in the Black Sea. We don't like it up here on Olympus much—not enough flesh, too much ambrosia, if you know what I mean." The bird ran a pink pointy tongue around its teeth.

"I'll give it a go," said Demon, opening Hephaestus's magic medical box for the very first time. Soft blue symbols glowed underneath the lid.

"State the nature of your beast's emergency medical problem," said a metallic voice.

"Um . . . ," said Demon.

"'Um' not a recognized problem of an emergency medical nature," said the box. "Does not compute with data program. Please restate." Demon took a deep breath. He wasn't used to boxes talking to him.

"Er . . . ," he said, stopping.

"'Er' not a recognized problem of an emergency medical nature," said the box. "Does not compute with data program. Please restate."

"Let me do it," said the head bird, hopping off the table and giving the box a peck. "I'm a Stymphalian Bird. My feathers have fallen out. I need new ones. Does that compute, you stupid square object?"

The letters under the lid glowed a sullen kind of green. "All right, all right," said the metallic voice sulkily. "Just having my little joke. Feather medicine coming right up, and I hope they itch terribly while they're regrowing." Immediately, a vial of bronze-colored liquid popped up in the center of the box. "Give 'em all one drop," said the box. "And mind those teeth. Should be fixed in about an hour."

Demon undid the vial and dripped a single drop into each bird's beak, careful to avoid slicing his fingers open. Sure enough, an hour later, all their bronze feathers had grown back.

"Thanks, Demon," they said as they flew off to catch the Iris Express down to their new home in the Black Sea. "We've left you a few old feathers on the side. They're useful for cutting stuff up. Or stabbing that Heracles if he shows his face up here."

Demon put the feathers away carefully in a drawer. "If that Heracles comes anywhere near my beasts again, I *will* stab him," he said. "Even if he does have muscles like tree roots."

"You're all right for a half-god human, really, Pan's scrawny kid," the griffin said to him. "At least you do seem to hate that horrible Heracles as much as we do."

Demon stroked its feathers.

"One day I'll give him what he deserves," he said. "No one treats my beasts like that." The griffin pecked him gently, only drawing a little blood this time.

"*Your* beasts now, are we? I wonder what Zeus will have to say about that, stable boy!"

But Demon found out just how empty his brave words were when Poseidon sent yet another one of Heracles's victims up to Olympus. The Cretan Bull had been stabbed in the heart, and its fire had gone out completely. If it hadn't been immortal, it would have been dead.

"HERACLES!" Demon yelled down the Iris Express as he hauled the bull onto his wagon with his silver rope. "I'm warning you! ONE more, just ONE more, and I'm coming down to sort you out."

There was no answer, but suddenly Demon

felt as if a hundred god and goddess ears were listening to him. It was not a comfortable sensation at all, and Demon had the feeling that once again, his big mouth might have gotten him into trouble. Nothing happened immediately, though, and Demon soon forgot about it in the commotion of treating his new patient.

CHAPTER 7

THE ETERNAL FLAME

Restarting the Cretan Bull's fire took Demon nearly a week. Back and forth, back and forth he went to Hephaestus's mountain, carrying load after load of hot coals from the forge. The poor creature was beside itself with rage, and if he hadn't had his magic silver rope to keep it tied down, it would have gored him at least a hundred times with its golden horns. It was not a cooperative patient at all.

"C'mon, bull," he pleaded as he tipped yet

another scoop of hot coals carefully down its throat.

It was no good. The bull's thrashing and tossing were gradually becoming weaker and weaker. All that was coming from its normally fiery fifth stomach was a wet sloshing sound. Demon couldn't think what to do. The magic box had mended the stab wound easily enough and had told him to fetch the hot coals—but the treatment wasn't working. He opened the box once again.

"State the nature of your beast's emergency

medical problem," said the now-familiar metallic voice.

"Same as before," said Demon. "I can't restart the Cretan Bull's fire. The coals aren't working. What else can I do?"

The box was silent for a moment, then the symbols under the lid began to flash orange, and there was a series of short beeps. A thin wavering tube appeared out of the box. It had a flat silver disk on the end. The tube swayed toward the bull, elongating as it went, and then the silver disk laid itself against the bull's fifth stomach.

"Diagnostics in progress," said the box. "Please wait." After a moment the tube whipped back into the box.

"Well?" asked Demon anxiously. "What did you find out?" *And why do you have to use stupid long words like "diagnostics"?* he thought, but didn't say because by now he'd found out that the box could be a bit temperamental if he wasn't polite to it.

"Diagnostics have detected a case of bovine pentagastric marine pyrosaturitis," said the box proudly. It sounded very smug. Demon bit his tongue to keep himself from shouting at it. He needed help too badly to annoy the stupid thing.

"Could you please explain what that is?" he said in his politest voice.

The box made a purring sound. "It means you've got loads of seawater in the creature's fire-making equipment," it said.

"Do you have a cure?" Demon asked.

There was a whirring noise as a small silver cauldron rose out of the lid and floated into Demon's lap.

"Beast patient will be cured by eternal

flame. Service does not provide eternal flame at present." The box snapped shut. It was a very final sort of sound.

Demon stood up, holding the silver cauldron. What he wanted to do was kick the magic medicine box, but curing his patient came first. Only he still didn't know how.

What do I do now? he thought as he fluffed up the silver straw around the Cretan Bull and made it as comfortable as he could. He decided to go and ask Hephaestus. Eternal flame sounded like the smith god's kind of thing. But when he got to the forge under the mountain, Hephaestus wasn't there.

"Gone to deliver two of my brothers to some mortal queen," said the gold-and-silver automaton robot that was keeping the fire going.

Demon's stomach slid down to somewhere near his feet.

"You, er, you don't have any eternal flame in here, do you?" he asked, all in a rush. Demon still wasn't used to talking to Hephaestus's metal people.

"Nope," it said, and it turned back to the fire. Hephaestus was right—the forge robot definitely wasn't one for talking much. Demon trudged back to the Stables. Perhaps the griffin would know.

"Eternal flame?" asked the griffin. "That's the stuff on Hestia's hearth. Why do you want to know? Do you need some or something?"

Demon explained about the Cretan Bull's waterlogged fifth stomach. The griffin just opened its beak wide and cackled. "Good luck with that. The last one to steal some was Prometheus—and as you know, he's currently strapped to a mountain having his liver pecked on a daily basis by our friend the Caucasian Eagle."

By now, Demon's stomach was past his feet and well on its way back down to earth. He went to check on the bull to see if, by some miracle, it was better. But it wasn't. He was going to have to go and visit a goddess he didn't know and ask her for a favor.

Goddesses weren't known for doing favors for anyone—let alone a stable boy. She'd definitely want something in return. Or maybe she'd be so grateful he'd gotten rid of the cow-poo smell that she'd give him the flame for free. He patted the bull. Too weak to do anything else, it groaned pathetically.

"I'll be back soon," he promised, keeping his fingers crossed. He just hoped it was true.

Althea the nymph agreed to show Demon the way to Hestia's palace. He felt very conspicuous and very small as he walked past the huge front doors of the other immortals. Althea was chattering away as normal, telling him who lived where, but he was too nervous to listen properly. Hestia's palace turned out to be right in the middle of all the other gods' dwellings.

"Will you come in with me, Althea?" he asked.

The nymph just giggled and shook her head, tossing her long, floaty hair.

"Nymphs are not allowed in the dwellings unless invited," she said. "And anyway, I've got some sunflowers to polish for Helios."

She flitted away, leaving Demon standing in front of a door carved with cooking pots and kitchen utensils. He raised his hand to knock, but the door creaked open before he could get his knuckles to it.

"Come in, little stable boy," said a deep voice. It sounded like cream and honey dripping onto hot rocks.

Demon forced his feet to walk forward. He

clutched his silver cauldron tightly as he went into a huge dark room. There was a fire right in the middle of it. Standing over it was a huge silver cauldron—an exact copy of the one he was carrying—hanging from a hook. There was a long-handled spoon in the cauldron, stirring all by itself. On the other side of the fire stood a figure. He fell to his knees.

"Oh, do get up and tell me what you want, Pandemonius," said the voice. "I'm not going to cook you. Yet."

Hestia laughed as a trembling Demon got up. "Only joking about the cooking," said the goddess.

Demon didn't believe her. But he couldn't think about that. He wasn't here for himself, so he cleared his throat and put on a brave face for the Cretan Bull's sake.

"I'm sorry to bother you, Your Goddessness,"

he said. "But would it be possible to have a tiny bit of your eternal flame? It's needed to cure one of the beasts in the Stables." He squeezed his eyes shut and crossed his fingers, hoping.

There was a rustle in front of him and a smell of *loukoumades*, the small honey cakes that were his very favorite thing to eat in the whole world. He thought of his mom mixing cakes and giving him the bowl to lick. A sudden rush of homesickness came over him. Why did he have to be up here with the stupid gods? Why couldn't he just go back to how it was before? Why couldn't his father have just left them alone?

Demon felt the little silver cauldron being plucked from his fingers. He cautiously opened one eye, blinked hurriedly, and opened the other eye. Then he remembered that he was standing in front of a scary cooking goddess. Hestia was examining the cauldron.

She was very tall and quite plump, and she was wearing an apron embroidered with pots and pans. She turned the cauldron around and around in her long, flour-dusted fingers.

"Hmm," she said. "You seem to have brought the right thing to carry the eternal flame, so I suppose I'll have to give you some. But there's something I want you to do first."

Demon's brain immediately went into a panic as he wondered what awful thing Hestia might be going to make him do. The smell of honey cakes was very strong in his nostrils now, and his mouth was beginning to water. He saw that Hestia was holding something small and golden out to him.

"I want you to try this and tell me if it's any good," she said. "It's a new recipe for the feast next week. Open up."

Demon opened his mouth in relief that his

task was so easy, and Hestia popped the small golden thing inside. There was a sort of explosion of sweet deliciousness on his tongue. It was the best honey cake he'd ever tasted in his life. He opened his mouth again. "More!" he demanded greedily, without thinking that it might be a bit rude to give a goddess orders. Luckily it was exactly what Hestia wanted to hear.

"Oh goody," she said, clapping her hands. "You like them."

Sometime later he left Hestia's palace, full to the brim and clutching the cauldron to his chest (plus a box of spare honey cakes). Hestia had given him a lid for the cauldron, to keep the eternal flame covered.

"Just don't let Zeus or any of the others see you with that flame," she said. "I got into terrible trouble the last time some of it went missing. I'm not supposed to let it out of the palace."

Demon promised. He tiptoed very carefully past all the palaces, trying hard to be invisible.

Upon returning to the Stables, Demon tipped the eternal flame carefully down the bull's throat. Just then he heard an appalling shriek. It went on and on and on, rising louder and louder and louder until it sounded like all the Furies rolled into one. The bull struggled to its feet as its fifth stomach caught light and started to roar like a furnace. He and Demon both realized that the shrieking sound was heading straight for the Stables.

CHAPTER 8

THE PEACOCK CHARIOT

Oh no, thought Demon. *Someone's found out I took the flame out of Hestia's palace.*

He ran up to the loft, hid under his blanket, and waited, shivering, to be turned into a little pile of ash. The shrieking stopped. He could hear banging and crashing noises below. Then there was silence.

"STABLE BOY! COME HERE!" said a voice.

It wasn't a nice creamy voice like Hestia's. It sounded like a thousand rusty knife blades clashing in a dark alley. Demon clenched his teeth to stop them from chattering and crawled out from under his blanket. He stiffened his jelly legs and made them climb down the wooden ladder. He could smell the fragrant breath of the unicorns floating up to him like a cloud of sweetness, and he wondered if it would be the last thing he ever smelled. Then he reached the ground and fell to his knees, mostly because his legs had turned to jelly again.

In front of him stood six peacocks, their jeweled tails spread out to hide the chariot behind. Demon's heart started to beat its way out of his chest. He didn't even have to see who was in the chariot behind the peacock tails, because he already knew.

Everyone had told him to keep out of Hera's way, and now here she was in his Stables. The peacocks hissed and bent their long necks toward him. Demon scooted backward hurriedly.

"W-w-what c-c-can I d-d-do for you, Y-y-your G-r-reat G-g-goddessness M-m-majesty?" he asked, just managing to get the words out. He couldn't believe he was still alive. Maybe she hadn't found out he'd taken the flame from Hestia's palace. Maybe her peacocks were just sick or something.

Hera climbed down from her chariot and walked around the birds to stand in front of him. Demon didn't dare to look up. He stared at her sandals instead. They were made of what looked like real gold rats' tails, and they had little onyx-and-ruby scorpions for buckles. Hera walked around him slowly. Demon felt her eyes pass over him like hot lava. Then she poked him in the ribs with her staff.

"Come with me, stable boy," she said. "I've got a job for you."

Hera strode back to her chariot, and Demon

somehow managed to get up and follow her. The peacocks pecked him as he passed them. It hurt, but Demon was too glad to be alive to care . . . and at least they hadn't drawn blood. He'd had much worse from the beasts in the Stables, anyway.

Hera thumped her staff on the chariot floor. "Sit," she commanded.

Demon sat by her feet, taking care to make himself very small and unobtrusive. Then, quite suddenly, the peacocks wheeled around and started to run. The chariot swooshed into the air, and the dreadful shrieking started up again. Demon sat on his hands to prevent himself from clutching at Hera's robe as they rose higher and higher and then suddenly plunged down with a stomach-sickening lurch, through the misty barrier and toward earth.

Where were they going? Was Hera taking

him home to his mom? Demon had about a millisecond's worth of hope before he remembered. The queen of the heavens had a job for him. Quite soon after that, the chariot thumped to a halt, and the shrieking stopped again. There was a smell of rotting eggs in the air, and something else . . . something that smelled like blood and fire.

Hera screamed. It was not a scream of fear, but a scream of rage. Demon clapped his hands over his ears, but it was no good. The scream got into every pore of his body. He felt himself begin to heat up. All the trees burst into flames and then died into small piles of black cinders that blew around in the angry breeze.

"Pleeease," he moaned, feeling the tips of his fingers begin to burn. The scream stopped abruptly, and Hera picked him up by the back of his slightly singed tunic.

"Look," she snarled, shaking him like a rat.

Demon looked as best as he could with his body being whipped back and forth. He sucked his sore fingers. Offy and Yukus were silent around his neck, obviously too scared to move.

Lying on the edge of a green and murky swamp was a truly hideous creature. It had nine charred neck stumps, none of which had a head attached. Eight of the obviously chopped-off heads were lying about on the blackened and trampled grass. The ninth head was nowhere to be seen, and the creature looked very dead. Hera flung Demon down and dropped to her knees.

"Poor little Hydra," she crooned, patting its thick green hide. "Did that nasty Heracles cut off your pretty heads, then? Never mind, my sweet, we'll get you all mended again."

She got up and turned to Demon, who lay wheezing and panting on the ground, trying to get back the breath she'd knocked out of him. Her voice was no longer crooning. The rusty knife blades were back.

"Mend my pet," she said. "Prove you deserve your job as stable boy, Pan's son, or I'll send you down to Tartarus as a snack for those revolting hundred-armed monsters quicker than you can say 'poo chute.'"

Demon had already struggled to his feet and was heading toward the horribly mangled beast. He began picking up heads and loading them carefully into the back of the chariot.

"Is this more of that horrible Heracles's work, Your Goddessness?" he asked, his hatred of the so-called hero making him brave enough to speak.

"Yes," said Hera. She looked sideways at the swamp, which began to boil, stinking even worse than it had before.

"Can't you do something about him, Your Goddessness?" asked Demon, who felt angrier than ever with Heracles at the state the poor beast was in.

He began stroking the Hydra's rough skin. It felt limp and cold, but he knew that would change up on Olympus. He remembered the griffin telling him on his first day in the Stables that it was only on earth that the immortal beasts could be "killed." He hoped that was true, or he was definitely going to be a hundred-armed monster snack. Hera snarled.

"Insolent stable brat. I'm trying. But Zeus insists that I play by his rules and set the vile wretch a whole lot of impossible tasks. Otherwise I would have blasted that lowlife hero from the earth already. I can't believe he got past my lovely pet alive—he must have had help from Athena. They'll both pay for that."

She pointed her staff at him. The lotus flowers on it spat sparks. "Now hurry up and stop wasting my time with impertinent questions."

Demon hurried. He wrapped his silver rope around the Hydra and with great difficulty dragged its mangled body over to the chariot. Then he heaved and dumped it, one leg at a time, on top of its heads. There was still one head missing, though, and Hera was tapping her foot ominously. The ground began to smoke. Demon ran from place to place, searching furiously, but it was no good—the ninth head was nowhere to be seen. He knew he was going to have to risk asking for help. He cleared his throat, which seemed to be full of thistle prickles.

"I'mterriblysorrytobotheryou, YourMajestic Goddessness, butIcan'tfindthelasthead," he said very quickly, before she could turn the staff on him again.

Hera didn't reply. She simply pointed her staff at an enormous rock, black with blood and soot. The rock exploded, and Demon threw himself to the ground as shards and slivers of sharp stone flew past him with a zzzzipping noise like a swarm of angry hornets. One gashed his cheek open, and he could feel the blood dripping down his face.

He looked up cautiously. Where the rock had been was now a hole, and in the hole he could see something glinting. He crawled over to it. There lay the Hydra's ninth head. It had a huge lump of glittering gold set right in the middle of it, just between the eyes. Demon reached into the hole and picked it up. Then he stood and placed it with the other eight heads in the chariot.

On the journey back to Olympus, Demon thought and thought as Offy and Yukus slithered over his cuts and bruises, healing him. How was he going to mend Hera's pet? Surely Hephaestus had said that chopping off something's head was fatal? And the Hydra had had all of its nine heads chopped off. That was probably nine times as fatal.

He just hoped the magic medicine box would help him. If it didn't, he was in big, big trouble. Being eaten by hundred-armed monster trouble, in fact. Demon didn't think he could possibly feel any more scared than he already did. But he reckoned that a trip down the poo chute to Tartarus might just do the trick.

CHAPTER 9

THE HYDRA'S FATE

The Hydra rested on the table in the hospital shed, hanging off the edges. It wasn't breathing much. There was just a pathetic-sounding wheeze from one of its throats every few minutes. Its heart didn't seem to be beating at all. All nine heads lay limp and listless. The bandages that attached them to its necks, although neat and tidy, were completely useless.

The magic medicine box had provided him with a huge pot of its usual wound-healing formula and a large paintbrush. Demon had done exactly what it had told him, but it was no good. Even after he'd fitted the right heads back on the right necks, the poor beast lay nearly as still and cold as when he had first seen it.

"C'mon, box. Please. There must be something else we can do," he begged it. But the box remained silent, its numbers now flashing a frantic red instead of the normal blue.

"Error message, error message, error message," it said over and over again in a high monotonous squawk. It was obviously baffled or broken.

As Demon shut its lid, he began to despair. He thought and thought, but by now he had done so much thinking that his brain just felt tired and full of nothing but fear and worry. Hera had gone back to her palace, but Demon could still hear her last words to him rattling around in his head.

"Remember, stable boy, find out how to mend my pet quickly. Or else." She had pointed her staff meaningfully in the direction of the muckheaps as the peacocks had started up their infernal shrieking again.

How long did he have before she came back to check on him? Did she even need to check on him? Maybe she could just watch him in some magic mirror. Demon shivered. He badly needed some advice, and he needed it at once, since the box was now useless to him. Did he dare leave the Hydra alone to go and see if Hephaestus was back? No. Perhaps he shouldn't risk it, just in case. He stuck his head out of the hospital-shed door.

"Althea," he called. "Are you there?" There was no reply. "Althea," he called louder. Still nothing. "ALTHEA!" he yelled. Almost at once the nymph floated around the corner of the building.

"All right, all right," she said. "Keep your eyebrows on. No need to wake up all of Olympus with your shouting. I was busy polishing Aphrodite's camellias for the party tomorrow, if you want to know. Now what is it this time?"

"Could you be a really, really nice nymph?" he asked, smiling his most appealing smile—the one that made his dimples appear and usually worked on his mom. Althea tossed her hair and pouted.

"Depends," she said. "Not if it involves offending Hera. I heard those wretched peacocks of hers screeching when they were here. She hates the nymphs enough already, and I don't want to be turned into a cow like poor Io was."

"It's only keeping an eye on the Hydra while I go and get Hephaestus," he said. "I don't want to leave the poor beast alone while it's in this state. I'll give you a whole box of Hestia's honey cakes if you do," he added temptingly. Demon knew perfectly well by now that nymphs loved anything sweet. They were always sucking nectar out of the flowers.

"Oh, all right, then," said Althea. "Hand them over." Demon ran up to his loft at once. It caused him a pang to see his precious *loukoumades* disappearing into Althea's mouth faster than a snake down a drainpipe—but he felt it was well worth losing them. "Yum!" she said indistinctly through a mass of sticky crumbs.

"Send the griffin to Heffy's mountain for me right away if there's any change at all," he said. "I'll be back as soon as I can."

Once again Demon was panting as he got to the forge. He dashed in. Hephaestus was definitely back, and Demon felt relief flooding over him. The fire was roaring higher and hotter than he'd ever seen it, and the smith god was banging away with his hammer at a large shield, which was glowing a fierce silvery-white with heat. The noise was indescribably loud.

"Hephaestus! Hephaestus!" shouted Demon, jumping up and down and waving to attract his attention. The automaton robot raised its head and reached out a silvery-gold hand to poke Hephaestus in the ribs. Hephaestus turned his head and saw Demon.

"GET OUT RIGHT NOW!" he bellowed urgently just as the forge flared into the shape of a ferocious-looking dragon head.

Flames billowed out of the dragon's roaring mouth and wreathed the whole forge area in silver-white fire. Demon jumped backward toward the door just in time. There was a smell of burning hair as his eyebrows and bangs

were singed right off. Then there was one last almighty BANG from the hammer, and the flames died down and retreated with an angry snarl. Hephaestus limped over to Demon, picked him up by the front of his tunic, and shook him till his teeth rattled.

"NEVER, NEVER come in when the forge is fired up in dragon mode," he shouted. "Didn't you see the notice?"

He flung Demon down in front of a large slab of slate. There was a picture of a fearsome dragon spouting fire carved onto it with a large skull and crossbones. It was all too much. Demon burst into angry tears. He couldn't help it. All the fear and worry boiled up inside him and erupted.

"There, there," said Hephaestus more gently. "Never mind. But I don't know what I would have said to your dad if you'd been burned to a crisp." At the mention of his dad, Demon's tears turned to a hot resentful rage.

"Why do you think he'd even be worried about me, anyway?" Demon screamed. "He just dumped me up here and left me. He hasn't been to visit ONCE, even though he promised. I wish I were DEAD. And I soon WILL be. And I don't CARE!" His nose was dripping snot, and he wiped it crossly with his hand.

Hephaestus picked him up, carried him inside the forge, and set him down on a table. Then he handed him a length of grimy cloth. "Stop shouting, blow your nose on this, and tell me what the matter is," he said, handing Demon a glass of ambrosia.

Demon sipped at it. It tasted as vile as usual, but it did seem to calm him down a bit. He blew his nose.

"It's the Hydra," he began, sniffing loudly and disgustingly. When he had finished explaining to Hephaestus about Hera's threat and how scary and horrid she'd been, and about how the magic box wasn't helping, he looked the smith god in the eye. "I don't think it *can* get better, really. You told me that chopped-off heads were impossible to mend. So I'm doomed to go down the poo chute, aren't I?"

Hephaestus scratched his head. "Not necessarily," he said. "I think I said *almost* impossible. Let's go and have a look at this Hydra of yours, and then we'll see."

CHAPTER 10

THE MYSTERIOUS TASK

"You do know that Hera's my mother, don't you,
Pandemonius?" asked Hephaestus as he limped
slowly toward the Stables.

Demon swallowed. He'd forgotten that. And
now he'd gone and said how awful and scary
Hera was to her very own son. He opened his
mouth to say he was sorry, but Hephaestus
was still talking, so he shut up and listened.
He couldn't be in much more trouble than he
already was, anyway, he thought.

"I know everyone thinks she's horrible and grumpy—and she is most of the time—but she has a kind side. Sort of. She made Zeus accept me back on Olympus after he'd thrown me down to earth and smashed my bones up, you know. And she does love her pets in her own grouchy way. I reckon this job of mending the Hydra is some kind of test for you. She could perfectly well cure the beast herself if she wanted to. So you need to use your brains—if there are any inside that thick head of yours."

He put out a huge hand and ruffled Demon's hair. Of course, Demon's brain immediately felt even more like mush than it had before. Thinking was something he'd already done a lot of, and he wasn't at all sure he could do any more, let alone the kind that would solve a Hera task.

Demon pushed open the door of the hospital shed and went in, Hephaestus following close behind. Althea was floating around the Hydra's heads, humming.

"No change," she said. "Now can I *please* get back to polishing Aphrodite's flowers? I've only got about a hundred more to do before supper, and I don't like the smell in here." With that, she flitted out the door, flicking a kiss at Hephaestus as she went. "Don't look so serious, Heffy," she called over her shoulder. "It doesn't suit your big sooty old face!"

The Hydra lay exactly where Demon had left it. The magic medicine box lay silent beside it.

"Doesn't look too good, does it?" Demon said. His voice was gloomy and sad—just like he felt, really. Hephaestus hobbled around the beast and poked it with a large grimy finger. The head with the golden lump in its center wheezed once.

"Not looking too brilliant, I agree. And

you say the box couldn't help?" Hephaestus reached over the Hydra's huge green belly and opened the lid of the box. Right away it started squawking its error-message refrain and flashing red. "Stupid thing," said Hephaestus, giving it a thump. "It's gone and caught one of the viruses it's supposed to cure. Hang on a minute." He took a large golden screwdriver out of his belt and poked about in the box's innards. It stopped squawking almost immediately.

"State the nature of your beast's medical emergency," it said in its normal metallic tones.

"Hydra with chopped-off heads still seems to be nearly dead," said Demon, hopelessly. It was pretty much exactly what he'd told it before.

The box clicked and whirred, its symbols now returned to their usual clear blue. Demon and Hephaestus waited. And waited. And waited. Finally the box made a clunking sound, and out of it rose a large empty golden bucket and a pot. The pot contained one very large apple seed and some golden-orange earth, which smelled slightly of cinnamon.

"One Hydra cure-all," it said in its usual smug way. And then it shut down, refusing to say another word.

"What on Olympus do I do with those?" Demon asked Hephaestus. He couldn't for the life of him see how one apple seed, an empty bucket, and some soil were going to cure a seemingly lifeless beast with no heads.

Hephaestus began to smile. Then he began to laugh.

"Oh, ho ho ho! Very clever. I see exactly what the solution is. That's one very clever box, though I say it myself."

"Well, I DON'T," said Demon, feeling angry all over again. He hated it when people (or, indeed, gods) laughed at him. It made him feel all stupid and young, like he was a baby or something. Hephaestus just grinned.

"Oh no—I'm not making it easy for you," said Hephaestus. "That would make Hera very upset with me indeed. That box has provided you with everything you need right there, so work it out, boy, work it out. I'll give you just two clues: Ask yourself what you cart out of the Stables every day, and remember what you know about Hera.

Good luck, and hurry up about it—my mother isn't exactly renowned for her patience!"

With that, Hephaestus limped off toward his mountain.

Demon stamped his foot. Then he looked at the Hydra, lying there all limp and pathetic and wheezy. The most important thing right now was to get it better and to get Hera off his back. He could be properly furious with Hephaestus after that, if he still felt like it. But what about the clues Hephaestus had given him? What was it that he carted out of the Stables every day? He paced around and around the Hydra, racking his mushy brain for ideas. Then he smacked himself on the head.

"Of course," he said out loud. "Beast poo. That's what I cart out of the Stables every day. But what on earth do I do with it? And how does it fit in with the apple seed and the soil and the bucket?" He continued pacing, trying to remember every fact he knew about Hera, but nothing seemed relevant. Then the griffin poked its beak around the door.

"Everything all right, Pan's scrawny kid?" Demon heard the griffin ask. "Everyone's getting a bit smelly and hungry, so I let myself out. You haven't been on the evening rounds and we miss your happy little face, not to mention your shoveling skills."

Demon felt guilty immediately. He'd been so busy trying to find a cure for the Hydra that he'd neglected all the actual living beasts in the Stables. He looked at the griffin.

"Do you think I can leave it on its own?" Demon asked, jerking his thumb at his many-headed patient. He still wondered whether Hera was watching him, somehow, but maybe the beasts could give him some clues about her, and that was more important at the moment. At least he would be doing something useful while he thought.

"What? Old Nine Heads? Doesn't look like it's going anywhere anytime soon," said the griffin. "C'mon. Hurry up with that ambrosia cake. I'm hungry enough to eat a half-god human." It snapped playfully at Demon's ear, deliberately missing him by a whisker.

Demon fed all the beasts, then he got his broom and shovel and the wheelbarrow and started to muck out. The familiar routine seemed to clear his head.

"Does Hera have anything to do with apples?" he asked the griffin as he swept up bits of glittering silver straw and shoveled them into the barrow.

"Well, she has a tree that produces the golden apples of eternal life, if that's what you mean," said the griffin. Demon dropped his broom and stared at the beast.

"What do you mean, eternal?" he asked. The griffin sighed and looked at him,

"E-t-e-r-n-a-l," it said, spelling it out very slowly. "Something that lasts forever. You know the kind of stuff. Immortality and all that. She's got a whole orchard full of them now."

Demon suddenly felt excited for the first time in what seemed like weeks.

"What exactly do Hera's apples do?" he asked, crossing his fingers and toes for the answer he wanted.

"Well," said the griffin, "according to the stories, if you eat a bit of Hera's apples, you can be cured of pretty much anything—even being dead." Its huge eyes widened slightly. "You're not thinking of going to get one to cure old Nine Heads, are you? Only she keeps her trees at the other end of the world, and they're guarded by Ladon, the dragon who never sleeps, as well as by endless armies of dryads. You'd never make it in a million years—not a little shrimp like you. Even that beastly Heracles had to lie and cheat to get some, and we all know he's pretty strong and ruthless."

Demon smiled at the griffin smugly. He knew just what the apple seed was now, and where it had come from, or he thought he did. He knew what the bucket was for, too.

"I don't need to go and get one," he said. "I'll just grow my own." The griffin gaped at him. It seemed to be speechless for once.

CHAPTER 11

THE DRYAD'S MAGIC

Demon had done enough gardening to know that an apple tree didn't normally grow and bear fruit in two minutes flat. However, Hera could come back anytime, and his need for a Hydra cure was more urgent than ever.

But he now had hope.

This was Olympus. Magical things could and did happen here. He filled the golden bucket with beast poo, grabbed the pot of soil and the apple seed, and went to find Melia the dryad.

Dryads were nymphs who knew all about trees, and he was pretty sure she'd be able to help him. Demon found her at last in the grove near the Iris Express, singing to some blue lemons. He held out the apple seed, the golden bucket of beast poo, and the pot of cinnamony soil.

"Do you know how I can grow an apple from this really quickly?" he asked. "If I don't get one really, really soon, Hera's going to chuck me down the poo chute to Tartarus."

Melia looked at him, her fingers flying up to her mouth. "Ooh, dear!" she said. "I heard she visited the Stables. What *did* you do to her?"

Demon explained. Then Melia took the seed, the bucket, and the earth from him. She sniffed at the earth. "Mmm. Very nice. Did you want a ripe apple, or will a green one do?"

"Ripe, I reckon," said Demon. "I don't want

to give the poor Hydra a bellyache on top of everything else."

Melia blew on a clear patch of ground at the edge of the orchard and dug a hole with her copper trowel. Then she started to hum a vague little tune. A small cone of dust erupted from the hole and hovered over it. Melia poured the bucket of beast poo in first, then added the soil. She mixed them together and finally dropped in the apple seed, which she poked down into the mixture with her finger.

The dust cone collapsed over it, filling the hole to the brim. Then Demon watched in awe as her humming got louder and deeper and, somehow, richer. A tiny green shoot erupted from the ground, and within seconds a small tree stood there.

"Wow!" Demon said, leaning forward for a closer look.

Melia flapped him away crossly with her free hand. She was using the other one to support the tree trunk. In minutes the tree had grown taller than Demon and was covered in golden leaves. One large deep red bud of blossom appeared on a low branch, then changed to an open flower.

After that, Melia started to dance. Around and around and around she went, humming her deep, rich tune (which now seemed to have dark, earthy words twining through it), until Demon felt as if his own feet were growing roots. The red petals floated to the ground and exploded with small pops as an apple began to form where they had bloomed.

It was like no apple Demon had ever seen before. It was perfectly round, like a ball, and it was the color of a fiery sunset streaked with gold. Demon closed his eyes and sniffed. The apple smelled of everything delicious and wholesome and desirable, and he suddenly wanted to taste it with every bit of his being.

"Hey!" said Melia. "Snap out of it!"

Demon opened his eyes and found that the apple was in his hand and touching his lips. She wrenched his hand away. "If you eat even one bite of that, you'll be immortal. That sounds good, but trust me, Hera will get Zeus to make you pay, over and over and over. Just think about poor old Prometheus. Do you really want to end up like that or with your brains being chewed by a basilisk for eternity—or something even worse?"

Demon dropped his hand to his side with an effort. He was clutching the apple so tight that it should have been bruised, but when he looked down at it, it was as perfect as ever.

"Now," said Melia. "You'd better get back to

that Hydra, and I'll have a word with this tree. I think it'd be happier as a more normal sort of apple, and a lot less dangerous. There's a reason Hera has her orchards at the other end of the world, you know."

As Demon walked away, she started to hum again, a different sort of tune, and when he glanced back over his shoulder, the tree's leaves were slowly turning to a greeny-bronze. He forced his hand to stay away from his mouth, but it was really hard. The smell of the apple was driving him crazy, and by the time he got back to the Stables, he was drooling with an impossible longing to taste it.

Only the thought of Prometheus, chained to his mountain rock, having his liver torn out forever and ever, stopped Demon from stuffing the whole fruit into his mouth and chomping down. He charged into the hospital shed at a run because he knew that if he didn't get this done, he would give in to the terrible temptation.

He dodged around the Hydra, slammed the apple down on the counter, pulled out a sharp knife from the drawer, and cut the apple into nine even pieces, which immediately spurted a stream of sticky golden juice onto the knife. Demon didn't even notice the tiny drip falling onto his little finger as he rammed one segment into each of the Hydra's nine mouths, carefully avoiding the rows of sharp pointy teeth.

Almost immediately, eighteen marble-like red eyes, each with a black slit in the middle, opened and began to roll around frantically. Nine throats breathed in nine wheezy breaths.

"Agghagghah!" said the head with the golden lump, which lay right in the middle of the others. "Gnoink!" said the other eight. Suddenly, the Hydra's heads all shot upright, its legs began to wave in the air, and it heaved itself over and off the table, which fell with a crash against Demon's hand.

"Ouch!" he yelled, stuffing his bruised right hand into his mouth. Immediately, he felt a wonderful sensation of warm, succulent coolness traveling over his tongue and down into his body. It was as if heavy golden sunlight had been squeezed over the light of a pure new moon and mixed with concentrated essence of rainbows.

He snatched his hand out of his mouth at once, but it was too late. He'd had the teeniest, tiniest taste of the juice of Hera's apple from his little finger. Was he now immortal? It didn't feel like it. But how could he find out unless he did something really stupid like diving off the Stables roof and seeing if he survived splatting into the ground or not? He felt a twitch around his neck and put his other hand up to touch Offy and Yukus.

"Am I different?" he asked them in a panicky whisper. "Am I immortal? Can you tell? Quick! Have a look!"

The two snakes untwined themselves and slithered up and down his body. It tickled, but Demon was too scared to feel anything but panic.

"Perhapsssss you sssseem a ssssmidgen more magical." The snaky nostrils sniffed inside his ears. "Yesss. There issss a ssssssmall shift."

"Will Hera notice?" asked Demon urgently. His poor heart was trying to beat its way out of his chest. There was a pause while the snakes did some more sniffing.

"We ssssssussssspect not," they hissed as they coiled themselves around his neck again. "The change is infinitessssimally ssssmall."

Demon wasn't entirely sure what "infinitesimally" meant, but his heart slowed down a bit. He just hoped Offy and Yukus were right, otherwise there would be worse than the poo chute in store for him.

The Hydra was now nuzzling him inquisitively with two of its heads. He noticed that it had very long curly eyelashes. Demon had expected it to be like Hera—bad-tempered and dangerous—but he was very relieved that it wasn't. He didn't think that he could have coped with being bitten by nine heads right now—it had been quite a tiring day, all things considered.

"Hey," he said, stroking the Hydra. "I'm glad you're mended—and not just because I didn't want to go down the poo chute to Tartarus. Now let's go and find a nice big pen for you to live in. Do you feel up to some ambrosia cake?"

The Hydra purred and rubbed up against

him again, nearly knocking him off his feet.

Just as Demon was settling the Hydra into its new home, Hera's peacocks shrieked their way into the Stables again. The Hydra poked its nine heads over the pen fence.

"Mommmmmy!" it called. This was the first time Demon had heard it say anything at all. It seemed to be a beast of very few words.

Hera rushed out of her chariot and over to the Hydra, gauzy shawls flying and bracelets rattling.

"Who's my little oochie-coochie pet monster?" she crooned to it.

Demon felt slightly sick. He usually shouted loud insults at anyone who used undignified baby language with animals, but he managed to keep his mouth shut by biting his tongue hard. His mom would have been proud of him, he thought,

and anyway, he wasn't risking Hera getting in a bad mood again. He let out a breath he didn't even know he'd been holding. She didn't seem to have noticed his slight shift toward immortality.

"You did well, stable boy," said Hera. "The hundred-armed monsters will have to do without their treat this time. In fact, I may even reward you. What would you like best? Jewels?" She gestured with her lotus flower staff, and a shower of glittering rubies, sapphires, and emeralds fell at his feet. Demon shook his head and tried to stop the Hydra from eating them. Hera flicked her staff again, and the jewels disappeared. "No jewels? What, then?"

Demon cleared his throat, wiggling his bitten tongue experimentally to see if it still worked. "I'd like some real food to eat, please, Your Goddessness. If that's all right," he added hastily.

"Oh, very well," said Hera. "I expect I can manage something. I'll talk to Aphrodite. She's in charge of catering this week, so any food you do get is likely to be fluffy and pink and wobbly." With that, she climbed into her chariot and flew off. Demon just got his fingers into his ears in time to avoid the worst of the peacock shrieking.

CHAPTER 12
THE FEAST OF THE GODS

The next morning, Demon was cleaning up after the Cattle of the Sun. He had a new helper in the Stables. The Hydra was following him around like a large, green nine-headed dog, carrying all his buckets and brooms and rakes in its nine mouths. It seemed to be very grateful to him for saving its life, though it still didn't say very much other than "nice Demon" and "more ambrosia cake."

Demon wondered if it was a bit simple in the

head after its ordeal. If so, it was one more thing to add to the long list of gripes and grievances he had to thrash out with horrible Heracles when they finally met. Demon's hand tightened on his shovel. He might not like eating ambrosia, but his muscles were definitely getting stronger. Maybe quite soon he might get the chance to hit Heracles once or twice before that big beast bully smashed him with that huge ugly club of his . . .

That was when the cherub arrived.

It cleared its throat crossly. "Message from Hera, Queen of Olympus," it said. "You are to present yourself at Zeus's palace tonight at the third thunderclap, stable boy." It fumbled in the pouch at its side. "Oh, and clean yourself up a bit before you put this on. You can't wear a filthy old rag to a feast with the gods, you know."

It handed Demon a brand-new white

tunic with a band of deep gold-and-purple
embroidery at the hem.

Demon was very nervous as the first of the
thunderclaps sounded. He walked hurriedly
toward Zeus's palace, not wanting to be late.
Melanie the naiad had let him use a corner of
her spring to wash in, and had even lent him
some of the shampoo she used on her own
blue locks and then brushed the tangles out of
his hair for him. Demon wasn't sure if he liked
smelling of watercress and buttercups, but she
assured him the goddesses would like it a lot
better than his normal Stables smell of straw
and poo.

The white, gold, and purple tunic felt softer
than anything he'd ever worn before, and
Melanie had found him a pair of new golden
sandals from somewhere. They felt strange on

his usually bare feet. The doors to Zeus and Hera's palace were wide open, and there was music and laughter coming from inside.

As the last thunderclap echoed right above his head, Demon walked in, hoping his stomach wasn't going to rumble. He was hungry enough to eat anything—even pink food if he really had to.

The gods and goddesses of Olympus were waiting for him. Zeus sat on a huge throne in the middle of them all, holding a sizzling lightning-bolt scepter. Demon recognized Hera and Hestia, and there was Hephaestus, smiling at him, dressed in white and not sooty for once. Demon dropped to his knees just as he spotted his dad at the end of the table, giving him an encouraging wave.

"Pandemonius, son of Pan," said a booming, thundery voice, which could only belong to the king of the gods. "Are you happy in your work?"

Demon dared to look up. "Yes, Your Great Majesty Godness," he said. "It's the best job in the world." As he said this, he realized it was absolutely true. Without really noticing, he'd grown to love his work in the Stables and the beasts who lived there.

"Then approach, Pandemonius."

Demon got up and walked toward Zeus's throne. For once he wasn't scared of being turned into a pile of ash. He kneeled at Zeus's feet, and the great god placed a wreath of golden laurels on his head.

"I name you Official Beast Keeper to the gods," Zeus said, "with responsibility for all the magical beasts in our realms, and those of our brothers and sisters. You will get seven golden Olympus tokens a month to spend as you wish, and you may attend four Olympian feasts a year. Now, let the celebration of our new Beast Keeper begin!"

As he spoke, lightning flashed all around the room, and several little gold-and-silver carts rolled through the doors, smelling of the most delicious things imaginable. Nymphs whisked in with pink-covered tables and couches, and several fauns danced about, playing jeweled flutes.

"Sit by me, son," said Pan, patting the pink couch beside him. So Demon did, and then Hephaestus came and flopped down on his other side.

"See," he said, grinning through his beard. "I knew there was a brain in that head of yours. Hera was amazed you worked her little test out, I can tell you."

"He's not my son for nothing," said Pan proudly, putting his arm around Demon.

And then the food arrived. What food it was! Dishes of roasted pigeons with yogurt and almonds, chicken and lemon soup, sweet figs and tart, creamy cheese, Hestia's delicious honey cakes, apricot tarts, fresh peaches and strawberries, exotic fruits and nuts from the ends of the earth. Some of the carts held food that was pink and wobbly and fluffy, as Hera had predicted, but there was so much else on offer that it was easily avoided. Demon ate and ate and ate till his tummy was like a tight little drum.

Tomorrow he might have to go back to horrible old ambrosia again, but tonight . . . tonight he would feast on Olympus as the one and only official Beast Keeper to the gods.

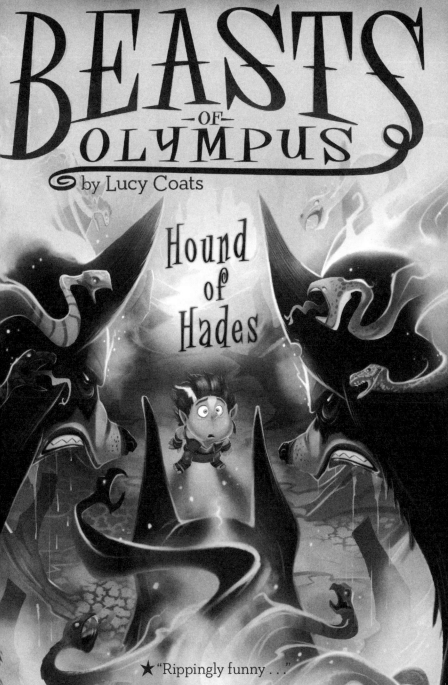

BEASTS
OF
OLYMPUS

by Lucy Coats

Hound
of
Hades

★ "Rippingly funny . . ."
—*Publishers Weekly*, starred review

BEASTS
OF
OLYMPUS

by Lucy Coats   art by Brett Bean

Hound of Hades

CHAPTER 1

OFFICIAL STABLE BOY TO THE GODS

Demon, son of the god Pan, and brand-new Official Stable Boy to the gods, had a bellyache.

It was a bellyache of monumental proportions. Even Atlas, the giant Titan, had never had a bellyache as big as this one, Demon decided.

He lay under his blanket in the loft above the Stables and wished he hadn't eaten those final ten honey cakes that the goddess Hestia had offered him as "a going-home snack." He was still so full after the gods' celebration feast that he hadn't slept a wink all night. The prospect of his usual early-morning task of shoveling barrowsful of poo down to the hundred-armed monsters in Tartarus was making him feel greener than moldy spinach. He groaned and turned over on his straw mattress, closing his eyes and wishing that Eos, the dawn goddess, would hold off on opening up the day.

"Hey! Demon! I'm hungry! Where's my breakfast?" came a loud shout from below. There was a scrape and clatter of claws on the ladder as the griffin popped its head through the trapdoor. It leaned over and poked its sharp beak into Demon's stomach.

"Go 'way, griffin," Demon moaned. "I'm ill. Very ill. In fact, I may die any minute."

"Huh!" said the griffin. "Well, I wouldn't lie around being ill and dying for too long. I hear from the nymphs that you're going to have an *important visitor this morning.* One who won't be too impressed with a lazy stable boy who HASN'T FED HIS CHARGES!" As the griffin yelled the last four words, he snatched the blanket away and nipped at Demon's bare toes till they bled.

"Ouch! All RIGHT! I'm coming." Demon leaped out of bed and threw on his old tunic. The two healing snakes who lived in his magical necklace, Offy and Yukus, set to work mending his poor bloody toes. It was an easy job compared to the dreadful wounds Demon had suffered since he started in the Stables of the Gods.

The magic snakes were soon done and slithered back up around his neck. "What important visitor?" he asked the griffin as he tied his silver rope belt around his waist.

"Aha!" said the griffin mysteriously, tapping one grubby claw against its beak.

"You are a very annoying creature some-times," said Demon. "Anyway, I don't have time to worry about some stupid visitor. As you so kindly reminded me just now, I've got work to do." But as he descended the ladder, a small nervous lump lodged itself in his chest somewhere just above his solar plexus. What if the important visitor was Hera? What if she had another impossible task for him to do? What if she threatened to turn him into a heap of char-coal? He could hear the griffin giggling to itself above him. That was never good news.

Demon headed off to clear out the muck

created by the Cattle of the Sun, make sure the nymphs had milked the unicorns, and feed leftover ambrosia cake to all the immortal creatures. By the time he finished, he had a pounding headache, and his stomach felt like a herd of man-eating horses was galloping around in it. Luckily his new friend, the nine-headed Hydra, had helped him out by carrying buckets, rakes, mops, and brooms for him in all its mouths. It also pushed the poo wheelbarrow with its tail.

"Thanks, Doris," he said as he tipped the last of the stinky mess down the poo chute. The monsters who lived below roared appreciatively. The Hydra grinned at him, its hundreds of sharp teeth glinting in the pale sunlight reflecting off Eos's pink fluffy bedsheets, hanging out to dry in the dawn sky. It loved having a proper name, and it was so grateful to Demon for saving its life that it would do almost anything for him.

"Doris likes helping," it said. Then it fluttered its eighteen pairs of long green eyelashes at Demon. "Snackies for Doris now?" it asked hopefully.

Demon tossed it a few bits of leftover ambrosia cake, and Doris retired to a corner of the Stables to chew on them. There was soon a spreading pool of drool beneath it—Hydras were messy eaters at the best of times. Demon headed over to the hospital shed to see if Hephaestus's magical medicine box would have something that would make his stomach feel better. It was meant for the beasts, really, but at this point he didn't care. He just wanted to feel normal again. As he opened the door to the shed, the comforting smell of aloe- and lavender-soaked bandages wafted out to greet him. The big square silver box lay on the table in front of him. As he lifted the lid, the familiar soft blue symbols sprang to life.

"State the nature of your beast's emergency medical problem," the box said in its metallic voice.

"It's not a beast. It's me," said Demon, rubbing his poor stomach and feeling very sorry for himself all over again. "I've got a horrible bellyache and a thumping headache, and I think I might die if you don't do something about it." He didn't say that the bellyache was from eating too many of Hestia's honey cakes.

A long silver tentacle with a flat disk on the end of it shot out of the box and snaked down the front of Demon's tunic. It was cold and made him jump. After a few seconds it retreated back the way it had come. "Error code 435. Human ailment. Does not compute with data program. Unable to assist. Thank you for your inquiry." The box closed abruptly, with a final, resounding click.

"Stupid box," said Demon, kicking the table so it rattled. The box opened a tiny bit, and a pointed silver tongue stuck out in Demon's direction. It made a very rude farting noise, then the box snapped shut again.

As Demon stormed out of the hospital shed, slamming the door behind him, he saw a swirling cloud of utter darkness burst out of a large crack in the ground. He was sure the crack hadn't been there five minutes before. The cloud raced toward the Stables at an alarming speed with a sound like a thousand hammers pounding. Demon's heart began to thump. This must be the griffin's Important Visitor arriving.

CHAPTER 2

THE IMPORTANT VISITOR

Demon reached the double doors of the Stables just before the thundering cloud of darkness did. He straightened his tunic hurriedly and ran his fingers through his hair, hoping there wasn't straw in it. A large, pointy-booted foot emerged from the inky murk. Demon caught a whiff of something strange. It smelled sort of damp and musty, like old, dead things mixed with the scent of burning hair. The foot was followed by a tall figure, cloaked all in black. In one gloved hand it carried a huge helmet, studded with bloodred rubies, and in the other a set of reins, which it tossed to Demon. The reins appeared to be attached to something (or somethings) within the blackness.

"Hurry up and ssstable those for me, dear boy," the figure said, its sibilant voice soft and dangerous. "And find them sssome meat, will you? That ussselesss sssatyr Sssilenusss tried to feed them leftover ambrosia cake lassst time I was here. They burned all the hair off his legs, as I recall." With that, the figure strode off toward Zeus and Hera's palace, leaving Demon staring openmouthed after it.

"He arrived then, I see," said the griffin into Demon's left ear, nearly making him drop his set of reins.

"Wh-who . . .
wh-what . . . ?" he
stammered. "Er, I
mean . . . who IS he?"
asked Demon, finally
managing to get
his words out
properly.

"That? Oh, that's Hades. Lord of the Underworld. Terror of Tartarus. God of death. Bit overwhelming, isn't he?" said the griffin. Then it sniffed. "I see he's brought those wretched things with him again," it remarked sourly. "His pride and joy, they are, but I wish he'd stick to horses. Better put them in the fireproof pens at the end. They nearly torched the place when they were here before. And as for what they did to poor old Silenus . . . it doesn't bear thinking about. He had blisters for months."

Demon gave an experimental tug on the reins Hades had thrown him. They seemed to be made of some kind of pliable blue-black metal, light but very strong. Whatever was at the other end roared and tugged back, and two huge jets of blue-white flame lanced out of the darkness straight at him. He and the griffin ducked and rolled out of the way just in time as five bales of the Cattle of the Sun's special hay frizzled into nothingness behind them.

"Play them your dad's pipes, quick!" yelled the griffin through the roaring. "Don't know if they work on earth dragons, but it's worth a try!" It scuttled around the corner of the Stables and disappeared. Demon hung on to the lashing, thrashing reins with one hand, while fumbling in the pocket of his tunic with the other. *Dragons?* he thought. *Dragons? DRAGONS?* His legs wanted to run one way and his frantically beating heart the other. He wrenched the Pan pipes out of his pocket, swung them to his lips with one swift movement, and started to blow. The cascade of tinkling notes dropped into the roaring flame, and immediately the reins fell limp in Demon's other hand. A crooning noise came from the darkness, and two vast scaly bronze heads slowly emerged out of the gloom. Their huge eyes were as big as Hera's golden dinner plates, and deep purple fires burned in their depths as the beasts walked forward. Their enormous taloned feet shook the ground at every step. Sharp spikes covered their bodies in unassailable armor, and drifts of ghostly pale smoke hung from their nostrils.

Demon blew the pipes for all he was worth, not daring to stop as he tugged the vast beasts toward the rock-walled pens at the very back of the Stables. He'd always wondered what creatures they were for. Now he knew.

If he'd thought getting dragons into their pen was hard work, unharnessing sleepy ones with one hand was almost impossible. He managed it eventually, using the spikes as a ladder, then throwing the undone metal straps outside the dragon pens for polishing. When he had finished, Demon walked out backward, slammed the fireproof gates behind him, and ran a safe distance before he plucked up the courage to stop playing.

There was a sudden blissful silence. Not a beast in the Stables was moving or making a noise. When he peeked into the griffin's cage, it was asleep on the floor, whiffling gently through its beak. All his other charges were the same. Even the giant scorpion was lying down on its back with its stinger curled up. Demon grinned, looking at his trusty Pan pipes.

"Thanks, Dad," he whispered. His bellyache had gone now, and his head felt clear. He'd survived. Again. But then he remembered the other thing Hades had asked him to do. "Meat. Where do I find meat?" he wondered. All there usually was to eat on Olympus was ambrosia cake. Except on feast days.

Feast days! That was it! Maybe there was some meat left over from last night's feast. He definitely remembered seeing some roasted ribs going past on Hephaestus's magical serving carts. He shoved his pipes into his pocket again and set out for the forge under the mountain. The smith god always gave him good advice.

Hephaestus was lying down on a rocky couch with a grimy blanket over him and a stained handkerchief spread over his head. One of his silvery-gold robot automatons was pumping the forge bellows gently, keeping the fire to a muted glow. It raised a metal finger to its lips.

"Sh!" it said. Hephaestus's robots never used two words where one short one would do.

Demon looked at the god of the forge. Was it worth the risk of waking him? Heffy wasn't the sort to turn a boy into charcoal, but you never knew with the gods. They could get nasty in a minute. Still, given the choice between Hades or Hephaestus being angry with him, he'd take his chances with Heffy any day. Demon drew in a deep breath and tiptoed over to the couch, ignoring the robot's attempts to hush him.

He coughed quietly; then, as there was no response from the sleeping god, a little louder. Still nothing. One grubby, charcoal-dusted finger poked out from under the blanket, so Demon bent down and tugged at it gently.

"Ahem! Hephaestus! Sir! Your Godishness! I wouldn't wake you, only it's a bit of an emergency . . ."

There was a snorting and a harrumphing from under the handkerchief, with a few indistinguishable words thrown in between. "Wassermatter . . . *snortle* . . . thoughtIsaidnovisitors . . . *harrumph* . . . owmyheadhurts . . . !"

Demon bent down and looked at the groaning god sympathetically. He knew just how Heffy felt. Just then Hephaestus sat up unexpectedly, beard all wild and snarly, eyes red-rimmed and half shut. His head met Demon's with a clash. Demon tumbled backward and into the robot, who fell over with a metallic crashing sound.

"AARRRGGHH!" roared the god, leaping up and dancing around the forge, head in his enormous hands.

"OOOF!" said Demon, a heavy metal foot clipping his shoulder as little bright stars of pain flared around his forehead.

"I THOUGHT I GAVE ORDERS THAT I WAS NOT TO BE AWAKENED!" Hephaestus shouted, sparks flying from his eyes and the tips of his fingers. The robot said nothing. It was too busy collecting pieces of itself and reattaching them.

"I'm veryveryvery sorry, it was all m-m-my fault," said Demon in a very small, shaky voice. He'd rarely seen Hephaestus angry before, and he wasn't sure he wanted to again. The god was batting at his beard, which was now on fire from the sparks that had landed in it.

"Zeus-blasted stable boy," said Hephaestus in slightly milder tones. "What's so Hades-bebothered important that you have to wake a god from his richly deserved beauty sleep?"

"Well," said Demon, "since you mention Hades . . ." He explained about earth dragons

needing meat, not ambrosia cake. "I don't want to get my legs burned off like poor Silenus did," he finished. "I don't think even Offy and Yukus could mend that."

Hephaestus stood there for a moment, pulling out clumps of singed beard and scratching his head while he thought.

"Hestia," he said finally. "She usually supervises cleanup after a feast. If there's any meat about, she'll know where it's kept. You can find her in the kitchens." He looked around. "Where's that wretched robot when you need it?" The robot stepped out from behind a pillar. "Here, you—take Demon to the kitchens. And put that arm on the right way 'round before you come back." He limped over to his couch and lay down again, sighing loudly. "Now go away and leave me to my headache."

CHAPTER 3
THE KITCHENS OF THE GODS

The robot led Demon through the winding back ways of Olympus and past places he'd never seen before. He hadn't realized that palaces had back doors with garbage outside them, nor that the gods and goddesses would need normal things like clotheslines. He ducked under a row of fragrant yellow spider-silk robes hung out to dry in the morning breeze. They smelled like soft sunshine and sweet flower petals as he brushed against them. Demon wanted to stop and look around, but the robot was setting a good pace with its long metal legs. Besides, he knew he had to find the meat for the earth dragons before Hades came back.

A little farther along, as they turned in to a white marble courtyard, a delicious aroma hit him square in the nose. It was both familiar and unfamiliar at the same time. "Mmm," he said, sniffing with his eyes half closed. What *was* that? It smelled good. Suddenly his stomach rumbled loudly. He didn't see how he could be hungry again after last night, but it appeared his stomach had different ideas.

"Kitchens," said the robot, pointing to an open wooden door. Demon thanked it, and it turned without another word and took off. He went up to the door and put his head around it, peering in. Inside was a pantry, with hundreds of dirty gold and silver dishes on every surface.

Almost as many jeweled goblets were piled up in heaps on the floor.

There seemed to be nobody around, so Demon picked his way through the chaos and went in. This was where the delicious smell was coming from. He saw a huge kitchen, bustling with activity. There were small cooking fires burning everywhere. Their light reflected off the gleaming sides of a thousand copper pots, jugs, and whole racks full of shining silver knives. Around the sides of the kitchen stood a series of long tables where nymphs were chopping and pouring and mixing. The air was full of the sound of sizzling. In the middle of it all stood the goddess Hestia. She held a large wooden spoon in her hand and directed the whole frantic cooking operation. She was wearing the same apron embroidered with pots and pans he'd seen her wearing when he visited her palace to get some eternal flame to cure the Cretan Bull's bovine pentagastric marine pyrosaturitis. Close by her, several fauns were wearing smaller aprons. They were working hard at frying large amounts of sizzling meat in enormous pans. Others were scurrying around, pulling trays of steaming bread out of huge ovens. One very small faun was standing on a stool beside Hestia, fanning her face with a large palm leaf. It was very, very hot.

"Ah! Our Official Beast Keeper has arrived," said Hestia. "Hello, Pandemonius. Would you like one of my special *loukaniko* sausages for breakfast? They're a brand-new recipe—I added cinnamon and apples to the mix.

All the gods and goddesses always want a home-cooked breakfast when they wake up after drinking Dionysius's silly grape juice." As she spoke, she whisked a sausage out of the nearest pan, grabbed a hot roll, slapped the meat into it, and handed it to Demon. The smell was divine. He bit into it, not caring that it was piping hot. It was utterly delicious, sweet and spicy and full of just the right amount of meat.

Oh no! Meat. He'd forgotten for a second.

"Yum!" he said hastily and indistinctly, chewing frantically. "Yum yum YUM!" He didn't want to hurry this. It would be back to horrid ambrosia cake soon. "Er, Your Goddessness, I was wondering . . ."

Hestia shoved another full roll into his free hand. "Try this one," she said. "It's got just a touch of pine nuts and wild thyme honey. Oh, and don't worry, I know what you've come for.

I saw Hades go storming past about half an hour ago. I suppose he was upset about missing the feast last night. Glaukos over there is already loading up some supplies for those wretched dragons of his." She pointed to a faun throwing large pieces of cooked flesh into a battered silver wheelbarrow.

Demon felt like falling to his knees with gratitude. Hestia was definitely the nicest goddess ever.

"Fank you," he mumbled around another mouthful of bread and sausage. Hestia just waved him toward the wheelbarrow, before turning to smack a nearby faun about the horns with her wooden spoon. There was black smoke coming out of the frying pan he was looking after.

"Use those tongs!" she yelled. "Did I say I wanted them burned to a crisp? I'll burn *you* to

a crisp if you don't CONCENTRATE!" Demon
hurried away. Hestia might be nice, but he
wasn't taking any risks.

All the beasts were still asleep when Demon
got back to the Stables, panting slightly from
pushing the heavy barrowful of meat. He tiptoed
up to the rock-walled pen and unlocked the
fireproof doors, Pan pipes at the ready just in
case. But both dragons were slumped on the
floor. Small streams of ghostly smoke
rose from their cavernous nostrils
as they snored. He quickly
tossed the meat into the
large stone trough

gouged out of the wall, hoping they wouldn't wake. He didn't want to be in the same place as two hungry dragons. They might see him as a tasty snack to finish off their meal. Sure enough, just as he was fastening the doors, there was a flash of flame and a great roaring and chomping noise. Obviously, like most beasts, dragons woke up at the smell of food.

He felt a sharp claw dig into his shoulder. "Saved me some meat, did you, Pan's scrawny kid?"

asked the griffin menacingly. "You'd better have." Clearly the dragons were not the only ones to have been woken up by the smell of food. Luckily there were a couple of small legs of lamb left. Demon tossed them to the beast, who caught them in his huge curved beak.

"Eat them quietly," he hissed at the creature. "Or they'll all want some." Most of the beasts survived on stale ambrosia cake. The more carnivorous ones complained about it dreadfully. He picked up the dragon harness and struggled to sling it over his shoulder. Although his muscles had become stronger with all the shoveling and brushing and barrowing of poo he had to do daily, the mess of metal straps and breastplates was very heavy. He hauled them out to the front of the Stables and sat down on a bale of golden hay. Using a bottle of Eternal All-Shine he'd gotten from Melanie the naiad, he began to clean and polish the disgusting, charcoal-crusted harnesses.

Twenty minutes later, the harnesses were shining like new, all ready for Hades's return. Demon just hoped he'd done a good enough job not to be turned into toast.

It seemed that he didn't have long to wait for the god of death. Just as he'd finished clearing away the clean white bones that were all the griffin had left of its meal, the bars of sunlight falling across the floor of the Stables faded and turned to gray. There was a sudden breath of must and mold in the darkening air. Before Demon could even turn around, a heavy hand fell on his shoulder.

"Ssso, ssstable boy," said Hades in his soft, hissing voice. "I sssee you haven't been eaten by my dragonsss. Yet." There was a sinister pause, and then he went on, his fingers digging in a bit, so Demon could feel the prick of his long nails. "My sssissster Hera tellsss me you're good at mending sssick beastsss. Are you?"

Demon didn't quite know what to say. If he said yes, it might sound like boasting, which he knew the gods didn't like.

"Well, Your M-m-mighty D-d-dark Goddishness, I wouldn't say *good*, exactly. I've had a lot of help from my father and Hephaestus . . . a-and a bit of good fortune with my cures." He kept his eyes firmly on the floor, hoping that Hades would just go away and leave him alone now that he'd answered. But no such luck. The god clapped him on the shoulder so hard that Demon fell to his knees.

"A modessst boy. I like that. You'll need to pack up your medical thingsss, ssstable boy. I need you in the Underworld for a while. I have a sssickly hound who needsss your attention urgently. Now, take me to my dragonsss. I have sssome treatsss for them." As Demon led Hades toward the dragon pens, his mind was whirling. How could he go down to the Underworld? Surely that was just for dead people. And who would look after the Stables if he was gone? He left Hades crooning to his dragons as if they were puppies, tossing strings of entrails into the air for them to catch. Then Demon took to his heels and ran as fast as he could to the hospital shed. As soon as he was inside, he scooped up some lavender and aloe bandages, which he stuffed inside his tunic, and grabbed his magical silver medicine box by one handle. The griffin poked its head through the doorway.

"Bad luck, Pan's scrawny kid. Word is you've got to go downstairs and visit with the Lord of Hell. I'd pack your warm cloak. Gets chilly down there, so I hear." Demon set off back to the Stables, the griffin loping beside him on its lion paws. Demon lugged the box behind him, bumping it over the rough earth as he ran. It let out an indignant squawk, and four short legs appeared at its bottom corners.

"Emergency locomotion program in progress," it squawked.

"Did I know you could do that?" Demon said, stopping dead in his surprise and letting go of the handle. The box bumped into him, knocking him over. "Ouch!" he said. His knees were going to be permanently scabbed at this rate.

"That box is full of surprises," said the griffin. "Heffy gave it some upgrades, remember? Now come on. Hurry up. You have dragons to harness, and it doesn't do to keep Hades waiting. Not the most patient of gods, old Hellface."

"But who's going to look after all of you?" Demon asked. "I'm supposed to be the Official

Beast Keeper to the gods, but how can I do my job properly if I keep getting taken away from Olympus by gods and goddesses?"

"Don't worry about that," said the griffin. "Doris will do cleanup if you offer it snackies of extra ambrosia. Beats me why it likes that disgusting stuff," it added gloomily.

A short time later, Demon had given Doris the Hydra enough extra ambrosia cake to keep it happy for days. It had given him loving licks with nine slimy green tongues and promised to keep the Stables clean till he returned. After that, he wrestled the harness onto two well-fed, happy dragons. He then led them up to the swirl of impenetrable black mist where Hades was waiting, tapping one pointy black boot impatiently. The box followed closely at his heels like a faithful dog.

"Hitch them up, ssstable boy, hitch them up,"

said the god of death. So Demon closed his eyes, tugged on the reins, and stepped forward into the darkness. As soon as the mist touched him, it felt like he was being sucked down into a pit of grief. All the sad things that had ever happened in his life swirled through his head at once. The time the baby chicks had fallen into the pond and drowned. The time he hadn't been able to save his favorite pet hen from the foxes. The time he'd found a wolf cub in a hunter's trap. His mother weeping over a patient she hadn't been able to save . . . He stood, frozen, the blue-black metal reins dropping unnoticed from his hand, tears pouring down his cheeks.

"Ah," said Hades. "I'd forgotten about the wretched ssside effect my pretty missst has on anyone who isn't me. Here, boy, put thisss on and don't lose it. You'll need it down below. And for Hermesss'sss sssake, wipe your nose.

I don't want boogersss sssmeared all over my niccce chariot." His gloved hand held out a ring made of shiny black stone. Demon fumbled it onto his middle finger, where it settled, seeming to shrink and cling like a small band of cold fog. Immediately the feeling of sadness lifted, and as it did, he noticed a chariot in front of him. Fixed to the back of its blue-black metal frame were two red lights in the shape of eyes. As Demon stepped closer, they swiveled around to watch him. The dragons backed themselves between the shafts, and Demon buckled the straps to hold them in. He patted them on their scaly shoulders and turned to Hades.

"All ready, Your Fabulous Formidableness," Demon said, wiping his nose with the back of a grubby hand and sounding almost cheerful in his relief at not feeling sad anymore. The god shuddered slightly and held out a black handkerchief.

"Revolting boy," he said, climbing into the driving seat. Demon started to follow him in, but Hades held up one black-gloved hand. "Nuh-uh, ssstable boy! No one travels with me. I'll sssee you down in the Underworld sssoon. Mind the ghosssts on your way in from the gatesss." With a malevolent grin, he cracked a whip of blue lightning above the dragons' heads, and immediately they plunged downward into the opening that had just appeared at their feet.

Demon stood staring in shock as the red eye-lights of the chariot vanished, and the opening snapped shut again as if it had never been. Did Hades really expect him to get to the gates of the Underworld all on his own?

Apparently the answer was yes.

CHAPTER 4

JOURNEY TO THE UNDERWORLD

"Oh," said Demon finally, his mouth hanging open. "But . . ."

The griffin cackled behind him. "Expecting a lift, were you, Pan's scrawny kid? Nope. You'll have to do it the normal way—get Charon the Ferryman to row you across the Styx and all that. Remember to take a couple of coins for him—and a couple for the way back, if you're lucky enough to survive. Go on, hurry up and hop on the Iris Express. She'll take you where you need to go. He wasn't joking when he said 'sssseee you sssoon,' you know." The griffin's imitation of Hades's snakelike voice was uncannily accurate.

Demon trudged back to his room to fetch the coins and then headed to the Iris Express. He was still followed by the box, which was staying remarkably silent. He forgot all about his warm cloak in his worry about what to say to Iris. He'd never summoned the gods' messenger before.

"Er, Iris Express, please. For me and my box. To go to the gates of the Underworld," he said nervously. There was a whoosh and a swish, and a rainbow arced down from the blue sky and landed in front of him.

"Unaccompanied minors and inanimate objects must belt up," said a tinkly voice from just above the rainbow as Demon stepped on. Immediately, multicolored bands looped themselves around him and the box, pinning them both so they couldn't move. Demon's heart began to beat very fast, remembering his last trip on the Iris Express. He closed his eyes and gritted his teeth, waiting for it to plunge earthward.

"Hold on, Iris," said a light, cheerful voice. "Wait for me." Demon opened his eyes. Standing in front of him was a tall, thin god with a mischievous smile on his face. Under one arm he carried a silver helmet. He had a strange carved staff in his hand, around which two golden snakes looped and turned in an endless figure eight. Demon recognized Hermes, chief messenger of the gods, and stood up as straight as he could while being strapped in.

"Good morning, Your Gargantuan Godness," he said politely.

Hermes laughed. "Hello, Pandemonius. No

need for the flattery. Just plain Hermes will do," he said. "I'm not one of those gods who likes all that boring bowing and scraping. Now, I hear old Hades has snaffled you for some important medical work. Hephaestus thought you might want a bit of company on the first bit of the road. Tricky place to get through, the Underworld. Especially since Heracles . . ." He scowled. "Well, anyway, we're all relying on you to fix things down there."

"Me? Fix things?" said Demon. He had a nasty sinking feeling as he asked the next question. "Uh, what exactly am I supposed to fix? Hades just said he had a sick hound. What's that horrible Heracles got to do with it?" Demon had a serious grudge against Heracles, who was always trying to kill the immortal beasts.

Hermes laughed again. "Sick hound? Oh, that's a good one. I never knew my uncle Hades had a sense of humor. The beast is certainly sick, but he's not exactly a hound. Anyway, you need to get there as quick as you can. I'm sure Hades will fill you in on what Heracles did when we arrive. Iris, take us down to that side gate no one uses anymore. It's the fastest way in."

With stomach-churning suddenness, the wisp of colored nothingness dropped downward, and Demon was suddenly concentrating too hard on not being sick to ask any more questions. Just when he thought he was going to lose the battle, there was a thump, the rainbow ropes loosened, and he fell forward. A strong arm caught him just before he hit the ground and set him on his feet.

"Here we are," said Hermes. "Welcome to the side gate of the Underworld—or Hell, as some of the northerners like to call it." They were outside the entrance to a very large cave. Long coils of green-gray moss and old spiderwebs hung from its top and all around the sagging iron gates on both sides, making it look like an old man's toothless mouth surrounded by straggly silver whiskers. Although the sun shone outside, dark fingers of mist reached out from the cave mouth and clung to Demon's and Hermes's feet. The fingers had covered the silver box almost entirely, when Demon felt them wrap around his ankles and drag him forward. Then the clammy fingers started to crawl up his legs.

"Hey!" he yelled. "Stop it!" He tried to run backward out of their grasp, but they clung even harder. He began to panic and thrashed around in his efforts to escape. Then the dank tendrils touched the hand wearing Hades's ring. Immediately the mist fingers shriveled and shrank back into the cave mouth.

"That's it," said Hermes. "Show

them their master's ring. Should get you in and out of most places down here. All we have to do now is get past the angry ghosts."

"A-a-angry ghosts?" Demon asked in a small voice. He didn't like the sound of that. "Couldn't you just take me straight to Hades, Hermes? Please?"

"Now where would be the fun in that?" Hermes said. "I'll get you past the ghosts, but then I've got to go and do a bit of business with some dead heroes. I'll give you one tip, though: Hephaestus told me to tell you that the box will help if you get into a tight spot. You just have to access the special features. Now come on. It doesn't do to keep Charon the Ferryman waiting. Follow me!"

With a playful hoot of laughter, he darted forward into the darkness. Demon followed at a run. He had no choice. Only Hermes knew the way. The sole comfort he had was the silver box waddling and hopping along behind him, special features and all. He shuddered, too scared to look back, and ran on through the twisting loops and turns of the steep passage. The god's staff gave out a faint greenish-gold light that reflected off the black stone walls. There was a familiar damp smell of dead things in the air, which got stronger and stronger the deeper into the earth they traveled. Demon could hear a roaring noise up ahead, and suddenly he and Hermes burst out onto the banks of the River Styx. Across the river was an enormous crowd of spectral gray shapes, howling and moaning. Some were flinging themselves into the water, but as Demon watched, the water formed itself into lips that sucked them in and spat them back onto dry land. Others were tearing at each other, ripping off arms and heads in a bloodless frenzy of viciousness. As each ghostly limb or head dropped to the ground, it rose into the air and reaffixed itself to its spectral body. These ghosts were clearly very angry indeed.

"D-do we h-have to g-get through THEM?" Demon stuttered. His legs and arms started to shake uncontrollably, and his heart was trying to climb out of his body. Being torn apart by furious ghosts while still alive would definitely be worse than being shriveled into a little heap of ash by a god, he thought.

"Yep," said Hermes cheerfully. "But don't worry. I have a trick or two up my godly sleeves."

Then he cupped his hands around his mouth. "Yo! Charon, you old lazybones. Get that ferry over here double-time. Two passengers bound for Hades." A long black boat materialized from the opposite bank. The ferryman's staff dipped in and out of the water without so much as a ripple. As the boat slid up beside them, Hermes leaped lightly over the bow and held out a hand to Demon. "On you get, young Pandemonius."

The boat rocked slightly as Demon stepped aboard, and then there was a thump as the silver box stumbled on behind him and fell heavily onto its side. "System reboot, system reboot," it said in a faint metallic shriek, blue sparks escaping from the slightly open lid.

The small legs retracted, and with a click and a hiss, the box fell silent. Demon had no time to worry about it, though, as Charon stood up and loomed over him, holding out a hand, palm upward. It was a long, bony hand, almost fleshless, with yellow nails like horny talons.

"Pay the ferryman," he croaked. Demon fumbled desperately in the hanging pocket inside his tunic and came out with two copper obols, trying not to touch the withered skin as he handed them over. Without another word Charon tossed the coins overboard into the river. As they sank beneath the surface of the still water, he pushed off with his staff. The shrieking ghosts drew nearer and nearer, and now Demon could see that they all had bloodred eyes and sharp, pointed teeth. Demon began to shake again. They were the scariest things he'd ever seen, and he didn't want to be anywhere near them. He gave the river a desperate look. Maybe if he jumped in and swam downriver . . .

"Don't even think about it, Pandemonius," said Hermes, giving him a sharp look and grabbing his arm. "The waters of the Styx do strange things to half-mortals. You wouldn't want to end up serving Hades forever as a ghostly beetle boy, now would you?"

Charon cackled. It wasn't a friendly sound.

"N-no," said Demon. "But I also don't want to go anywhere near those horrible ghosts. Why are they so angry, anyway?"

"They're the souls of the murdered dead, seeking a way back into life to get revenge on their unpunished killers in the upper world," said Hermes, letting go of him. "Can't blame them, really, poor things, but I agree they're not very nice. Now, grab hold of the end of my staff in one hand and that box in the other, and be ready to move as soon as we hit the bank. We'll need to be quick."

Demon bent down to grab the handle of the box, which lay still and dead in the bottom of the boat. "Any special features would be welcome right about NOW," he said hopefully.

The box woke up immediately, beeped once, and began to flash silver and blue. "Initiating solo pteronautics mode," it said in its annoying tinny voice. Just as Demon tugged on the handle to try to lift it, it shot up off the floor of the boat, suddenly light as a feather, pulling his arm up with it, so Demon dangled from one hand, legs kicking in the empty air beneath him. Large, bright blue wings erupted from the box's sides, flapping frantically as the box listed to one side under Demon's weight. The handle he was holding glowed bright red, and he let go with a yell and dropped heavily to the deck, sucking his burned fingers.

"Error code 781. Passenger mode disabled," it beeped at him as he lay there, slightly stunned.

"Quick," shouted Hermes again, his voice sounding frantic. "Grab my staff." They hit the bank with a jolt, and the angry ghosts began to swarm aboard. Charon beat them off with his staff, laying about him left and right as he knocked them over the sides. Without even thinking, Demon launched himself at Hermes's staff and seized it in both hands. The golden snakes wrapped themselves around his wrists. Suddenly he and Hermes were zooming upward, following the blue trails of sparks coming out of the now-flying box. Demon felt an icy cold hand wrench at his bare ankle, and then it was gone and they were soaring over the heads of the angry ghosts. Wails of rage followed them for what seemed like miles. Then, quite suddenly, they vanished. Demon, Hermes, and the box soared downward toward a barren landscape of pure silver-gray. The god's sandals were just above Demon's head. He saw that, like the box, they had wings, white ones with golden tips. As Hermes landed, Demon noticed an earthshaking noise far off to his left. It sounded like something was sneezing its head off. A ginormous something. At each sneeze, the ground trembled under his feet, and afterward a dreadful howling filled the air.

"What's THAT?" Demon asked.

"THAT is your new patient," said Hermes.

"It definitely doesn't sound like a hound," Demon said apprehensively. Anything that shook the earth when it sneezed was not going to be like any dog he'd ever come across, that was for sure.

"Told you it wasn't," said Hermes. Then he sniffed the air. "I'd better be going now. I smell the lovely graveyard whiff of my uncle, and he doesn't really approve of me. Not much for fun and jokes, old Hades. The palace is that way." Putting a hand on Demon's shoulder, he pointed to a small uphill path between the rocks. "So long, kid. We're all counting on you. Oh, and remember, whatever happens, DON'T EAT ANYTHING DOWN HERE." Then he put on his silver helmet and disappeared. Demon was all alone in the Underworld, and the silver box had just flapped over the horizon.

CHAPTER 5

THE GUARDIAN OF THE UNDERWORLD

Demon set off at a run, scrambling up and over the pale rocks. Now he, too, could smell the unmistakable reek of death wafting toward him on the still air. As he reached the top of the hill, he saw an extraordinary sight. Immediately below him stood a vast palace, built of smooth black granite flecked with silver, each tower, turret, and spire crowned with a rotating silver skull with ruby eyes. On each side of the palace stretched walls so high that he couldn't see over them. And there, lying chained in front of a massive pair of closed silver gates, was a beast unlike any he'd ever seen. Each of its three gigantic dog heads was crowned with a hissing mane of colorful snakes. It had a dog's body, a serpent's tail, and sharp golden-clawed lion's paws. Hovering near it was the winged box, and beside it stood Hades, glowering like a furious black cloud.

"*A-AA-A-A-AA-A-CCCCHHHHHOOOOOOO! AAARRRROOOOOOOO!*" Each of the beast's heads sneezed and howled over and over again in a thunderous chorus. They thumped and thudded on the ground, so that cracks were appearing all around where it lay. It was clearly exhausted.

"You're late, ssstable boy," Hades growled. "Come here NOW." Stumbling and sliding over the trembling ground, Demon forced his wobbly legs to take him toward the angry god. If the poor beast hadn't been there, he might have turned and fled. However, the sight of it lying on its side, sneezing its three heads off, and the sudden worry about what Heracles might have done to it made him braver.

"I-I'm sorry, Your High Hellishness. I got here as soon as I could." He dared to look up at Hades. "What is this beast, Your M-m-m-majestic M-mightiness? And what's the matter with it?" *At least it's still visibly alive and has all its heads attached,* he thought.

Hades looked a tiny bit less angry as he heard the obvious concern in Demon's voice. But not much. Steam was drifting out of his ears, and his eyes were glowing red.

"Thisss," he said, "is Cccerberusss, my Guardian Hound of the Underworld. That oaf Heraclesss

beat him up in a fight. Then he put a diamond chain around his neck and dragged him up to earth. He'sss never been the sssame sssinccce. It'sss all my wretched sssisssster Hera'sss fault for giving Heraclesss sssuch a ssstupid tasssk. Now my poor hound is USSSELESSS." He spat, and where the spittle landed, it hissed and smoked. Demon cringed. He really, really didn't want to be in the middle of a fight between a scary god and an even more terrifying goddess. But then Hades beckoned him closer, and as Demon edged toward him nervously, Hades snapped open a small window in the silver gates. "Look through here, ssstable boy, and sssee what happensss when the Underworld has no Guardian." Demon peered through and gasped. Far away, on a plain covered in white flowers stretching as far as the eye could see, were thousands and thousands of figures. They were not just ghosts (though there were masses of those) but a few real live humans, too. The humans were wandering around, pointing and chattering, behind a man with a red placard on a stick.

"That idiot Heraclesss left the upper gate open. Now we have LIVING HUMANSSS HERE!" His voice rose to a roar, which made the ground tremble. "There'sss a man called Georgiosss running TOURSSS! 'Meet Your Favorite Hero' is how he'sss ssselling it up there on earth. And Brother Zeusss has forbidden me to do ANYTHING about it till YOU make Cccerberusss better!

"He won't ssstop sssneezing and howling. And he'sss doing it ssso loudly and ssso often that the foundationsss of my kingdom are SSSTARTING TO CRACK!" He gestured toward the largest rift. "Sssee, ssstable boy?" he hissed.

Demon looked, trying to keep his balance as Cerberus sneezed and howled again and the ground swayed like a ship's deck underneath his feet. The rock at the bottom of the cleft was moving, too, almost as if it was a barrier someone was trying to get through.

"I-it doesn't look good, Your Hellish Hugenosity," Demon said timidly.

"DOESN'T LOOK GOOD!" Hades roared. "That'sss Tartarusss down there! TARTARUSSS!"

Demon nearly let out a terrified squeak. He already knew that Tartarus was where the horrible hundred-armed monsters were imprisoned. The ones who'd tried to defeat the gods. The ones who ate all the poo from the Stables.

Hades bent his head closer. "You sssee the problem, ssstable boy," he said in a scary whisper. "If thossse hundred-armed monssstersss essscape, they'll dessstroy the whole world. Sssooo . . ." There was an ominous pause. Demon closed his eyes and braced himself. He pretty much knew what came next when a god was this angry.

Hades seized Demon by the shoulders. "You've got until the end of the day to find out what'sss wrong with my Guardian, ssstable boy, and cure him," he hissed. "Or I assure you, I'll put you in a worssse pit of flamesss than Ixion and roassst your toesss to cccinders. That'sss jussst for ssstartersss. After that I'll let my army of ssskeleton ghossst dragonsss chassse you and eat you over and over again for the ressst of your wretched mortal daysss . . . which I can make as long as I pleassse! How would you like THAT?"

Before Demon could answer that he wouldn't like it at all, Hades threw him to the ground with a thump and strode off into the palace. He slammed its black stone doors behind him with the sound of a funeral bell. Demon lay there, wheezing, trying to get his breath back. Offy and Yukus slithered off his neck and curled around his bruises, soothing them so that he was able to get to his feet again.

Wretched gods, he thought, not daring to say it out loud in case Hades heard him. Why did they always have to be so violent? He'd have tried his hardest to cure poor Cerberus anyway. Did Hades really think that threatening him with such awful punishments was going to help? He sighed, trying not to think of how roasted toes and being eaten by skeletal dragons would feel, and went over to his patient. Cerberus's three noses were red and running with yellow slime, and his eyes were swollen shut. The snakes that made up his manes sneezed continuously in a

faint hissing chorus, punctuated by enormous
volcanic *ah-choos* from
the three heads. Demon
stroked his rough fur.

"Poor old fellow," he said. "We'll get you
well again." Cerberus just groaned weakly
in between sneezes and howls. Then Demon
turned to the box. "I need you," he said, "and
none of your stupid word games. This is an
emergency." The box flapped over and settled

down beside him. Demon opened its lid, and the familiar blue symbols glowed up at him. "Tell me what's wrong with this beast dog," Demon commanded it. At once three cotton swabs on strings flew out. Working quickly, they rubbed around the six nostrils and took samples of the yellow slime, then retracted, disappearing in a flash of silver light.

"Running diagnostics . . . running diagnostics . . . running diagnostics . . . ," said the familiar metallic voice. Then there was a pause and a loud whirring sound.

"Tricephalic helionosos," said the box in its usual smug way. Demon felt like kicking it.

"Stupid thing," he said, too angry to be polite. "I TOLD you not to do that. Say it so I can understand."

"Sun," said the box, quickly flapping out of his way.

"What do you mean, 'sun'?" asked Demon. "Sun isn't an illness, is it?"

"Do I really have to spell it out?" sighed the box. "Patient is allergic to Helios's rays in all three heads. Must have had too much exposure when he was up top with Heracles. It's given him a permanent case of sneezes and earache, as well as swelling his eyes shut. He can't see, he can't hear, and he definitely can't do any guarding."

"Well, we need to cure him," said Demon. "By the end of the day. Or I'll be eaten by skeleton ghost dragons forever and ever."

The box buzzed and hummed. Then it buzzed and hummed some more. The blue symbols flickered.

"Come ON," said Demon. He looked over at the door of Hades's palace. He had the uneasy feeling that something horrible was going to come out of it at any minute. "Hurry UP!"

The blue symbols turned a vile sickly green, and a small crystal bottle rose out of the box's depths.

"Temporary stasis cure. Apply one drop on each eyelid and in each nostril," it said tinnily.

Demon seized the bottle, hurried over, and started to do as the box had told him. The drops smelled like honey. As soon as he had finished, Cerberus heaved three huge sighs, rolled over, and stopped breathing. Demon nearly stopped breathing, too.

"WHAT HAVE YOU DONE, YOU STUPID THING?" Demon yelled. The box flapped hurriedly out of the way as he frantically felt the unmoving beast's chest for a heartbeat.

"Bought you time," the box squawked sulkily. "That's what a stasis potion does. It'll keep the patient in limbo and stop him from sneezing for a while. That'll just about give *you* time to get the ingredients I need to make the real cure before Hades comes after you."

"Ingredients? What ingredients?" asked Demon. The box clicked, then spat out a piece of parchment with brightly colored pictures on it at Demon's feet. He bent and picked it up.

"Great," he muttered. "Three mysterious yellow petals, a fingerful of spiderweb, seven grass-of-Parnassus flowers, the toenail of a hero, a maiden's sigh, the high and low notes from a lyre—and a Cauldron of Healing." As he looked at the impossible-sounding list, Demon's heart sank lower and lower.

He dropped down to the ground despairingly beside Cerberus's still body, put his head in his hands, and groaned. He might as well call Hades to toast his toes now and be done with it. But just then, a cautious whisper came through the small window in the silver gates.

"Pandemonius! Pandemonius. Are you there?"

Demon raised his head. Only the gods called him Pandemonius—and his mother, when she was mad. Maybe Hermes had come back to help him. He got up slowly and went over to the gate, not daring to hope. When he peered through the window, he saw nothing except some wisps of white mist. Maybe Hermes was still wearing his invisibility helmet.

"Who's there?" he whispered back. "Hermes, is that you?"

"No, silly, it's me, Orpheus."

Demon frowned. There'd been an Orpheus his mother had told him about—some musician boy who'd defied Hades for the sake of love. Demon still couldn't see anybody, though, as he peered through the small gap.

"Where are you?" he asked. Gradually the wisps of mist formed into a shape right in front of his eyes—the shape of a teenage boy, carrying a musical instrument under his arm. A musical instrument? Could it be? Demon stared hard. It had a curving frame like two cow horns, with strings in between them. "Is that really a lyre?" he asked eagerly.

"Yes," said Orpheus, still a bit see-through, but now fully visible. "It is. Now come on through the gate. Quick, Pandemonius! I don't want Hades to catch me here!"

"Er, it's Demon, really," said Demon. "'Pande-monius' makes me feel like I'm in trouble."

"Well, you WILL be if you don't get through that gate RIGHT NOW!" Orpheus whispered urgently.

CHAPTER 6

THE BOY WITH THE LYRE

Demon was worried about leaving Cerberus by himself, but the box assured him that the Guardian of the Underworld would come to no harm.

"What if Hades comes out and sees him like this?" Demon asked, hesitating.

"Then you're better off not here, aren't you?" said the box in its metallic voice. "Now HURRY UP. Like Orpheus said, the clock is ticking, and you only have the rest of the day to find my ingredients."

A few moments later, Demon walked through the silver gates, closing them gently behind him with a last look back at his enormous beast dog patient, who hadn't so much as twitched a claw since having the potion. The box came flying up behind Demon, and together they met the ghostly figure pacing impatiently amid the white flowers. The red-eyed silver skulls on top of the palace swiveled to watch the two of them walk out onto the plain and then turned away.

Now Demon was truly in the land of the dead. He checked his body to see if it was still solid and human. Luckily it was. Then he took a deep breath and got a good look around for the first time. The dim twilight covered the landscape, making everything soft and blurred, as if it were not quite real. The sky (if it was a sky) had no clouds, stars, nor moon, but glowed eerie green as far as the eye could see. There were no birds overhead, only ghostly bats. The white flowers covered the ground like a carpet.

"How did you know I was here?" he burst out. He was really longing to know whether Orpheus could still play the lyre in his present form, but hesitated to ask. He'd never had a conversation with a ghost before, and he didn't want to say the wrong thing.

"Hermes said you were down here and might need a bit of assistance. Though I'm not sure how I can help, really."

Demon sent a barrowload of thankful thoughts in Hermes's direction. "Well, I can think of one thing right away," he said. Never mind politeness. "Does your lyre still work?"

"Of course it does," said Orpheus, sounding slightly offended, as Demon had feared he would. "I may be dead, but I'm still the world's

greatest musician, you know." He pulled out the instrument and strummed his fingers over the strings. The loveliest trill of music rose up into the air as Demon hurried to explain about his impossible list and about the two lyre notes he needed to help cure Cerberus.

"But how will you catch them?" asked Orpheus.

"Oh," he said. It simply hadn't occurred to him that he might need to actually catch the notes. He looked down at the box. "Any clever ideas, oh mighty chest of wisdom?" he asked it.

The box didn't answer. It just stomped over to Orpheus and shot out a long tube with a trumpet-like attachment, which fastened itself to the misty lyre like an octopus's sucker.

"Play a *D* and an *E*," it instructed
Orpheus.

The musician plucked two
strings. The first thrummed so low that
Demon felt it vibrate deep in his belly
button. The second was so high that it set
his back teeth on edge. As the two notes
died, the trumpet thing made a slurping noise
and gave a satisfied burp.

"Musical items retrieved and saved to disk,"
said the box as the trumpet detached itself
and slipped back inside the lid. *One ingredient
down, five more and a magic cauldron to go,*

Demon thought. Suddenly his stomach began to rumble loudly, and he realized he was hungry. It seemed like a very long time since he'd had those sausages on buns in Hestia's kitchens.

"Oh dear," said Orpheus. "I'd forgotten humans need food. That's too bad."

"What do you mean?" Demon asked.

"Well," said Orpheus, "you mustn't eat anything down here. That's how Hades caught his wife, Queen Persephone. She only ate seven pomegranate seeds, and now she has to stay down here for four months of every year. You can't let even one thing pass your lips until you return to the upper world, or you'll be Hades's prisoner forever."

Demon suddenly remembered that Hermes had told him the same thing. He decided to ignore his stomach, however much it complained. He definitely didn't want to be

Hades's prisoner for one single minute, let alone forever.

"Now show me that list," said Orpheus, holding out his insubstantial hand. Demon took it out of the folds of his tunic and handed it over at once. Unfortunately, the piece of parchment slipped right through Orpheus's fingers and drifted to the ground. Demon picked it up and held it out so that Orpheus could see the pictures.

"Hmm. Spiderwebs are easy. Arachne has lots. And grass-of-Parnassus grows by the banks of the River Lethe, just where it joins the marsh. I'm not sure about this yellow flower, but Eurydice is sure to know."

"Who's Eurydice?" Demon interrupted. Orpheus's see-through cheeks took on a slightly pink shade, as if Eos had just touched him with her fingers.

"Er, she's my girlfriend," he muttered. "Hades

is always forbidding us to be together, but we don't take much notice . . . that's why I don't want him to catch me." He cast a very nervous glance back at the silver skulls on top of the palace. "Anyway," he said, changing the subject quickly, "let's start with the hero's toenail. That shouldn't be too hard. There are at least a thousand of them down here, and it doesn't say it has to be a live hero, does it?"

"No," said Demon, "it doesn't. But where—?" He broke off, suddenly noticing that the crowds of people and ghosts he'd seen when Hades had made him look through the window of the gate were drifting toward them over the plain. There was a lot of noise going on, and the sound of a man shouting. "Might there be a hero in that bunch?" he asked.

"Almost certainly," said Orpheus. "Follow me. And try not to get trampled in the crush."

He shot forward, the bottom half of his body dissolving into mist as he did so. Demon sprinted in his wake, with the box galloping clumsily behind.

Demon felt a bit nervous. He hadn't met a hero before. Were they as scary as gods and goddesses? *Surely not*, he thought. Heroes were supposed to be good, weren't they? Then he remembered Heracles. Heracles called himself a hero, so maybe that wasn't true, after all.

Just then, Demon reached the crowd and crashed hard into the tall man called Georgios whom Hades had pointed out earlier. Up close he had a very large stomach and enormous, extremely dirty feet. All thought of heroes was knocked out of Demon's head as he tripped and landed with a bump, right on top of the box.

"Oof! Operating system overload! Operating system overload!" it squawked, spitting blue sparks. Demon got up hurriedly. He couldn't afford for it to break. There was no Heffy down here to fix it.

"What's this, what's this?" said a loud voice above him as he struggled to his feet. "I don't remember you being on my tour. Have you sneaked in without paying? Can't have that, can I?" said Georgios, waving his red placard.

"No," said Demon, indignant at the accusation. "I haven't. I'm on a job for Hades, if you must know."

The man laughed. "A likely story," he said. "A little shrimp like you on a job for His Majesty, the god of death? I don't think so, sonny. And what's that you've got there? Stolen it, have you?" He reached down for the box, but as his fingers touched it, it let out an orange flash of lightning, which made the man snatch his hand away with a shriek.

"Oops! Error code 93. That wasn't supposed to happen," said the box. It didn't sound very sorry, though. Demon felt like patting it, for once.

"Perhaps that'll teach you to believe people when they're telling the truth," he said. Georgios backed away, sucking his burned hand. He gave Demon a nasty look, waved his red placard over his head, and walked off muttering. Then he began to shout again.

"Move along, people! Move along! Follow Georgios's Underworld Tours sign! Best and only one in the business! Next stop, Achilles and Ajax." A chattering crowd fell in behind the man as Demon began to look for Orpheus. There was such a press of ghosts and people around him that he couldn't see the musician boy at all. He began to panic, but then caught sight of a misty lyre, held up high over everyone's heads, waving wildly. He began to run toward it, pushing his way between ghostly figures. They melted and flowed around (and sometimes through) him as he went, leaving him cold and shivering. He wished he'd remembered his cloak. Finally he got through to Orpheus.

"We'll never find anyone in this crowd," shouted the ghost. "Georgios's tours are making the Underworld a nightmare. Come this way!"

After more pushing and shoving, they came to a dead tree where several warrior ghosts wearing armor and carrying swords were gathered. With them was a gigantic man with a bow on his back, a belt made of faintly shining stars, and a mass of ghostly hounds at his feet.

"There's your hero," said Orpheus.

"Is that *Orion*?" whispered Demon. Orpheus nodded, so Demon marched up to him bravely. Orion had been killed by the giant scorpion,

Demon's least favorite beast in the Stables. Although Orion was a hunter, and he didn't normally like hunters, Demon had some sympathy for him. Demon had been stung by the giant scorpion, too. It hurt a lot.

"Excuse me, Your Extreme Heroicness," he said. "But could I have one of your toenails, please?"

All the warrior ghosts laughed. "You human souvenir hunters!" one of them said. "Bits from ghosts never last up in the mortal world, you know!"

"I'm not a souvenir hunter," said Demon angrily. "I'm the Official Beast Keeper to the gods. It's for a potion to cure Cerberus."

"Ah," said Orion. "Poor old Cerberus. We heard what happened. It's been chaos down here ever since. Well, if *that's* what it's for, you can certainly have one, Beast Keeper."

Orion shooed the ghost dogs away, bent down to his left foot, and pulled one of his large square toenails right off, making ghostly blood ooze onto his sandal. Immediately, a pair of pincers came out of the box and grabbed it.

"Toenail item recovered," it trilled happily.

"Thanks, Orion," Demon said gratefully, trying not to look at the misty blood pooling under the hero's foot. Then he had a thought. "Um, do you know where we could find a maiden's sigh, by any chance?" he asked. Orion and the others snickered.

"Orpheus here will help you with that," Orion said, winking. "He's got a few maidens sighing after him."

Orpheus blushed again. "Shhh!" he said. "Stop teasing me. You know there's only one I care about. Come on, Demon, let's go and find Eurydice."

Just four things to go now, Demon thought as they walked away from the laughing warriors. Maybe he could do this in one day, after all.

It took ages to reach the grove where Eurydice lived, but they got there at last. She was a tall, beautiful ghost with long hair down to her knees. Getting her to sigh into the box's trumpet attachment was easy. She just had to look at Orpheus. Demon stared at the two of them in disgust while they hugged and kissed as if they hadn't seen each other for years.

He didn't get this being-in-love thing at all.

"Ahem," he said at last, clearing his throat loudly. "Spiderwebs? Yellow petals? Grass-of-Parnassus? Cauldron of Healing?" The two lovers took absolutely no notice of him, gazing into each other's eyes goopily.

"I STILL NEED FOUR THINGS TO CURE CERBERUS!" he yelled at last. Both Orpheus and Eurydice jumped a foot into the air and then dissolved into streamers of mist.

"Don't DO that!" said Orpheus's voice indistinctly. "I thought Hades had caught us for a minute. Now we'll have to disentangle ourselves."

Tapping his foot impatiently, Demon waited while the two lovers sorted themselves out. "Now," he said. "Are you going to help me find the other things or not?"

CHAPTER 7

THE SPINNER'S CAVE

"Ooh!" said Eurydice, clapping her ghostly hands as she looked at Demon's list. They made no sound. "That's Cerberus's new flower!"

"Cerberus's new flower? What do you mean?"

"The wolfsbane petals. It was when Heracles was dragging him back down here from earth," said Eurydice. "I was coming out of Arachne's cave, and I saw it. Wherever his drool touched the ground, little yellow flowers sprang up, just like buttercups. They were so pretty. I've never seen a color like that down here before. It's all horrid old gray and black and that icky green sky."

"Could you take me there?" Demon asked eagerly.

Eurydice made a face. "It's a long way. And Arachne was quite mean to me last time I visited."

"We need to get spiderwebs from Arachne, anyway," said Orpheus. "She's only mean because she has all those arms and legs now. And we can take the shortcut past Lethe's marsh. Come on, it's important. Like a hero's quest or something."

"Please," begged Demon. He was very aware of the clock ticking away. He wriggled his toes uncomfortably.

"Oh, all right," said Eurydice. "I don't mind

Arachne really. But don't blame me if Lethe gets you. She's scary. We'll have to try to go past very quietly without her noticing."

Sometime later, Demon was trying to ignore his grumbling stomach as they trudged along in silent single file along a squelchy gray path beside a marsh. He was so hungry he would have eaten dirt if someone had given him a plate of it. *Don't eat, don't eat* was the monotonous refrain that accompanied his heavy footsteps. There was almost no one around in this part of the Underworld, apart from the ever-present ghost bats. Demon liked bats. There'd been a colony near his home in Arcadia. As he craned his head upward, trying to listen to what they were saying, he tripped over his own feet and fell into the marshy water on his hands and knees. There was a sudden stink of old, unwashed socks.

"Ugh," he spluttered. Just as he began to scramble out, a bony hand grabbed his wrist, nails digging into his flesh like claws.

"Not so fast," said a harsh voice, bubbling up from the water. Eurydice moaned with terror and hid behind Orpheus, who was holding his lyre like a weapon. Demon shook his wrist over and over again, trying to get free, but it was no good. The hand had him in an iron grip. Then the marsh plopped and bubbled as a terrible figure rose out of it, draped with slimy gray waterweed robes.

"What do we have here?" she snarled through a mouth full of sharp pointed teeth. "A half-mortal boy, two ghosts, and"—she peered over Demon's shoulder—"a silver box with legs?"

Demon's heart was pounding like one of Hephaestus's hammers. This must be Lethe, spirit of forgetfulness. "I-I-I'm sorry, Your

Magnificent Marshiness," he stuttered.

Lethe smiled at him. It was not a nice smile.
"Ohhhh! You WILL be," she said.
"You'll be sorrier than a squashed
scorpion." She began to pull him
down into the marsh. Demon
felt himself begin to sink.

"Noooo!" he wailed.
"Orpheus, help
me!"

Right then Orpheus began to play his lyre. Then he began to sing. It was the saddest song Demon had ever heard. As the sorrowful notes wove around them, Lethe's grip slackened, and Demon scrabbled backward toward the path. Fiery blue tears started to run down her cheeks and set the oily surface of the water aflame.

"Ahh!" she sighed. "Now you've spoiled all my fun, Orpheus. You know I can't resist your music." Orpheus kept on playing as Demon hauled himself out and tried to scrape off the gray ooze as best he could. When Orpheus's song came to an end, Lethe took a gliding step toward them through the burning water. Demon cowered. Eurydice was right. She was very scary, indeed.

"Oh, do stop cringing, boy," she said irritably. "Tell me why you were creeping past my marsh like a thief in the night."

Demon explained about Cerberus, his voice still trembling.

"Very well," said Lethe. "For Cerberus's sake I will let you pass this time. But if you ever come this way again, I shall demand a price. I will take your most precious memory from you. It will not be a pleasant experience."

Demon nodded. He would have agreed to anything to get out of there. He'd just noticed that the sky had grown a little darker. How long did he have before his day ran out? Then he noticed that Lethe was holding a bunch of delicate five-petaled white flowers out to him. "You may need these," she said.

Behind him, the box opened its lid. "Insert floral items here, please," it said, more polite than Demon had ever heard it. It was the grass-of-Parnassus that Demon needed for the potion, and now there were only three things left to find!

As they left Lethe behind, Eurydice was full of how brave and clever Orpheus had been. She went on and on about it as Demon stumbled up the high rocky hills that led to Arachne's cave. He wished she'd shut up, but he knew he needed her to show him Cerberus's flowers, so he didn't say so. Finally, as they came over one more summit, he saw a bright patch of yellow on the hillside below.

"That's them!" Eurydice cried when they were about halfway down.

Demon raced down the hill, almost slipping in his eagerness, picked three yellow petals, and brought them back to the box, which was ready and waiting beside Orpheus and Eurydice.

"Insert fl–"

"I know," said Demon. "Insert floral items here. I'm not stupid, you know."

"Could have fooled me," muttered the box

crossly, trailing along as they climbed higher and higher up the mountainside. Suddenly, Demon began to feel a stickiness under his feet. *Schlurp schlap schlurp* went his sandals. He looked down. Trails of thick slime covered the path.

"What's this?" he asked.

"Hush," said Eurydice. "You'll soon see. But don't mention it in front of Arachne. She doesn't like to talk about it." The stickiness got worse as they reached the entrance to Arachne's cave, and now Demon could hear a regular clicking and clunking coming from inside.

Orpheus rang a little bell by the entrance.

"Who's there?" said a silvery voice.

"Orpheus and Eurydice," said Orpheus. "And we've brought someone to see you."

"Come in then," said Arachne. "And mind the tapestries."

As Demon stepped into the cave and saw what was inside, his eyes nearly bugged right out of his head. There crouched an enormous gray spider, her eight legs busy weaving on four different looms, shuttles flying faster than his eyes could follow. There was a mass of different-colored thread spooling out from her spinnerets, along with a lot of sticky stuff that covered the whole floor with a thick, gluey coating. What was even odder was that the spider had the face of a pretty girl.

From each loom hung beautiful tapestries of all the gods and goddesses. There was Zeus with his thunderbolts, there was Hera, and there was Heffy at his forge.

The pictures were all slightly irreverent, though. Zeus was wearing a silly hat, Hera was sitting backward on a donkey, and Heffy was using a chicken instead of a hammer.

"Wow!" Demon said. "They're amazing! You must be very brave to weave *those*!"

It was just the right thing to say. Arachne beamed. "Ooh!" she squealed. "How nice of you to say so." Then she frowned. "But how does a mortal boy come to be down here?"

Demon explained about Cerberus yet again. "All we need now are some spiderwebs," he said. "And a Cauldron of Healing."

"Help yourself to webs," said Arachne, gesturing with one spindly leg to the corner. "I have plenty to spare." So Demon gathered up handfuls of the multicolored thread, getting himself hopelessly stuck together as he did so. The box clearly didn't like having sticky feet, so it had taken to the air again, wings flapping. Orpheus and Eurydice huddled away from the gusts of air, trying to hold their bodies together, as two long mechanical arms appeared under the box's wings and unraveled Demon, turning him around and around as it made the web strands into a neat rope.

"Web item retrieved and stored to memory," its tinny voice said.

"Did you say you needed a Cauldron of Healing?" Arachne asked when he was slightly less stuck together.

Demon nodded. "Do you know where I could find one down here?"

"We-e-e-lll . . . ," said Arachne slowly. "I'd normally send you up to Chiron the centaur in the mortal world. But down here . . ." She shook her head, and Demon's heart sank into his sandals again.

"Do you think Queen Persephone might have one?" Orpheus asked. "She's a healer, isn't she?"

Suddenly Eurydice started jumping up and down. "You're so clever, Orphy! I think I've seen one in her chambers," she squealed. "That time Hades made me be her lady-in-waiting, remember? She made a potion in it to mend one of the Skeleton Guard's arms."

"D-does that mean I have to go into Hades's palace?" asked Demon, dreading the answer and wondering nervously what a Skeleton Guard was.

"I'm afraid it does," said Orpheus. "And I don't think you've got much time left. Look!" He gestured at the cave entrance.

Demon looked outside. It was much darker.

"Two hours three minutes and twenty seconds, two hours three minutes and nineteen seconds, two hours three minutes and eighteen seconds," the box chimed in helpfully.

Demon glared at it.

"Let's get going, then," he said through gritted teeth.

CHAPTER 8

THE PALACE OF DEATH

It was one of the most uncomfortable journeys of Demon's entire life. The box had grudgingly agreed to enable its special passenger mode for him. It even provided a large bottle for Orpheus to pour himself into so he didn't blow away during the ride. After many tearful farewells from Eurydice, who was staying to visit with Arachne for a while, Demon lay across the box's silver lid. He clung on to Orpheus's bottle with one hand and the handle with the other. The large blue wings flapped frantically, once, twice, three times, and then they were airborne.

"Good-bye, Orphy!" sobbed Eurydice.

"Good luck, Demon!" called Arachne.

Demon slipped and slid from side to side, terrified that he was going to fall off as the box labored across Lethe's marsh and veered sharply right.

Then it plunged downward, avoiding a cloud of ghostly bats.

"*Ow! Ow! Ow!*" Demon howled as his toes scraped along the ground. The box merely let out a stream of blue symbols that roared past

his ears, crackling and spitting with sparks.
It rose unsteadily into the air again with an
unbalancing wobble that nearly caused Demon
to drop Orpheus's bottle. Over Eurydice's grove,
over the warriors' tree, over the crowded plain
of ghosts they flew, until Demon could finally
see the black walls of Hades's palace. With one
last mighty effort, the box heaved itself and
Demon over the silver gates and flumped down
beside Cerberus's body with a crash. As Demon
thudded to the ground, the silver skulls on top
of the palace roofs swiveled to look at him. Their
fiery eyes suddenly ignited, pinning Demon in
the middle of a circle of hot red beams.

"Intruder alert! Intruder alert! Intruder alert!"
shrieked the skulls, their bony jaws creaking like
rusty hinges.

"Quick!" said Orpheus's muffled voice from
inside the bottle. "Show them your ring!" Demon

got his hand out from underneath him and waved Hades's black ring at them. As soon as it touched one of the red beams, they all winked out.

"False alarm! Stand down, boys!" said the nearest skull. Demon looked around nervously. Had Hades heard them? He hoped not. He jumped to his feet, wincing at the pain from his rough landing. How much time did he have left before the god came after him? He HAD to find that cauldron quickly.

Offy and Yukus were just slithering down his legs and starting to mend him when he noticed all three of Cerberus's noses twitching.

"Oh no," he said to the box. "I think he's going to—"

"AAHHCHHOOOOO AAHHCHHOOOOO AAHHCHHOOOOO AAAAARRROOOOO!"

The three heads crashed to the ground,

making it shake and shudder. A deep new crack snaked out underneath them, and out of it came the sound of a thousand hungry hundred-armed monsters.

"Box!" shouted Demon. "Do something! Please!"

The silver lid flew open and the silver disk on a tube shot out, attaching itself to Cerberus's heaving chest. It then retracted into the box like a whip, and the box snapped shut.

"Sneezing symptoms should not have resumed yet. Running emergency diagnostics," it shrieked. Demon clenched his fists, trying not to panic. The snakes of Cerberus's manes were beginning to sway and stir. Then the box lid lifted again. A large glass tube with a thin pointy quill on one end and a ring on the other popped up from its depths.

"Inject patient's heart with contents of syringe," squawked the box. "Hurry!"

Demon didn't understand. "What do you MEAN?" he screamed.

"Stick him with the pointy end and push!" Its metallic voice rose to a screech. So Demon grabbed the glass tube and ran over to Cerberus. He felt desperately for his heartbeat as he saw the six nostrils twitch again ominously.

Thuddity thud thuddity thud! There it was. He jabbed the pointy end between the ribs and pushed down on the ring, which slid down into the tube with a hiss. Cerberus's body jerked once and then lay still again. Demon sat back on his heels, listening nervously to the furious bellowing coming out of the crack to his left.

"Emergency averted," said the box smugly. "You have precisely one hour to complete your task." The blue symbols inside flashed twice, and then the lid shut with a bang. "Battery recharge pending. Shutdown imminent." It sighed deeply, made a strange pinging sound, and went totally silent.

"Nooooo!" Demon yelled, shaking it by both handles and rattling the lid. "You can't go to sleep NOW!" But the box remained a lifeless silver lump. Nothing Demon said or did would wake it up. Finally, almost speechless with terror and frustration, he remembered to let Orpheus out of his bottle.

"What am I going to DO?" he asked as the mist flowed out and re-formed into his ghostly friend. The box had been his savior so often that he didn't know how he was going to manage without its tinny advice.

"Steal the cauldron, get back here quick, and hope it recovers," said Orpheus. "Didn't you hear it? We have less than an hour. Come on!" He flowed toward the black stone doors of the palace, Demon running beside him. One touch of Hades's ring on the doors and they opened. They were in!

Edging around the sides of a large courtyard with a dead weeping willow and a sluggish fountain in the center, Orpheus put a finger to his lips.

"This way, I think," he whispered, leading Demon into a wide passageway lined with unmoving giant stone skeletons that stared silently at one another across the shiny marble. Demon looked at them uneasily as he tiptoed past, but they didn't move a fingerbone. His thumping heartbeat ticked away the seconds as they ran up narrow black marble staircases and down broad, empty corridors. Then, just as Demon smelled the scent of new-mown hay—surprising in that musty place—they heard the sound of muffled marching footsteps.

"Quick! Behind here!" Orpheus hissed,

disappearing into an alcove behind a black velvet curtain. Demon slipped in with him, feeling the clammy mist of the ghostly body touch his side. He peeked out through a tiny crack to see a terrifying sight. A whole platoon of the giant stone skeletons had come to life and was marching in perfect step down the corridor, bones clicking softly as they passed.

"What are THEY?" Demon whispered, though he feared he knew. Immediately, the skeletons stopped dead, skulls turning toward the alcove as one. Demon froze, not daring to move even an eyelash, let alone breathe. Seeing nothing, they marched on, rows and rows of them. Demon let out a whooshing breath as the last of them disappeared.

"Phew!" he said.

"Definitely phew! Those were Hades's personal Skeleton Guard," Orpheus replied.

"The ones Eurydice was talking about. We passed the spares on the way. Didn't you notice?"

"I thought they were just statues," Demon said. Then he smelled the new-mown hay again. The scent seemed to be coming from a door just ahead. A door with a silver crown and a wheat stalk over it. "Hey! Are those Queen Persephone's chambers?" he asked. She was the goddess of spring and growing things, after all, as well as Hades's wife.

"Yes, they are. Wait there! I'm just going to make sure there's nobody inside," said Orpheus, flitting across the corridor. Demon jiggled from foot to foot impatiently, but soon Orpheus was beckoning him forward.

"Coast's clear," he said. "I think they're usually in the big hall at this time of day, judging the dead. Either one of the gods is on your side, or you're very lucky!"

Demon sent a quick thought of thanks to Heffy, Hestia, and Hermes, just in case. If any gods were going to be on his side, they were.

Queen Persephone's chambers were a riot of color, festooned with flowers so bright that they almost hurt Demon's eyes after all the gray and black. He suddenly realized how much he missed Olympus and the Stables. Were his beasts all right? Was Doris the Hydra cleaning out the poo properly and feeding everyone? But there was no time to think of that. The clock was ticking, and they needed to find that cauldron urgently. Demon and Orpheus moved quickly through the rooms, searching. Eurydice hadn't been able to remember exactly where she'd seen it. "There were pretty berries near it, I think," she'd said. "Red ones like lots of tiny cherries."

There wasn't a berry in sight in any of the

rooms. Not a single one. Demon was in despair, looking under drifts of poppies and behind clumps of bluebells.

"We'll never find it," he groaned. Even the normally cheerful Orpheus looked glum.

"It's all spring flowers in here," he said. "Maybe my Eurydice got it wrong."

Suddenly Demon had an inspiration.

"What if Queen Persephone had her autumn decorations up when Eurydice was here?" he asked. "This definitely looks like spring, but tiny red berries come in autumn from trees like mountain ash and hawthorn. Maybe we should be looking for those kinds of blossom." So they searched every tree in the place. There was cherry blossom and apple blossom, pear blossom and plum blossom, but they couldn't find a single hawthorn or mountain ash. Demon was about to tear his hair out with frustration, when his eyes fell on a little tree with shiny reddish bark and clouds of tiny white flowers, half-hidden behind a high wall covered in ferns. Between its moss-covered roots was a glint of gold. Demon ran over and pulled at it with a shout of triumph. Out came a tiny cauldron with a silver handle.

"Got it!" he cried. Just then there was a tremor beneath his feet, and a muffled rumble. "Oh no! I think Cerberus has started sneezing again! RUN!"

CHAPTER 9

THE CAULDRON OF HEALING

Demon and Orpheus ran at top speed back the

way they'd come, avoiding more

marching Skeleton Guards by the skin of their teeth, and burst out through the black stone doors again.

"Box! Box! Wake up! I've got the Cauldron of Healing!" Demon shouted, just as three enormous sneezes and howls shook the earth again.

The box woke up with a screech, glowed blue, grabbed the cauldron from Demon with its mechanical arm, and scuttled toward Cerberus. "Implementing potion interface, implementing potion interface," it gabbled, vibrating so fast that it became a silver blur.

With a burst of foul gas, several scaly green arms erupted out of the crack in the ground near Demon's feet. "AARRGGH!" Demon screamed, jumping for cover behind Cerberus's huge body as the arms grabbed at him. Orpheus slipped in beside him as a smudge of mist.

"What's happening?" Orpheus shouted. There was no time for Demon to answer. Instead he pointed with a shaking finger at the black doors, which had just crashed open. A whole platoon of Skeleton Guards came pouring out, stone swords raised, and started hacking at the scaly arms. Green blood poured over the dusty ground, smoking and bubbling, and the roars turned to shrieks of agony as more arms reached out from the cracks.

Demon was trying hard not to panic amid the chaos happening around him. He watched the box like a hawk, willing it to hurry. After a moment, the box snapped open, and then the small golden cauldron was floating up out of its inside, filled with a liquid that glowed bright purple.

"Patient must ingest potion immediately, patient must ingest potion immediately," it beeped loudly. Demon seized the cauldron by the silver handle and started pouring the purple liquid between each of Cerberus's three jaws in turn.

"Don't sneeze, don't sneeze, don't sneeze," he muttered over and over again as he worked faster than he ever had before. As Cerberus slobbered and dribbled and swallowed, the yellow oozy slime miraculously disappeared from around each of his six nostrils. He opened his suddenly unswollen eyes, got up, and shook himself, making Demon roll hurriedly out of the way of his enormous lion's paws. Three huge

heads gazed down at him. Three huge tongues lolled out between hundreds of sharp white teeth, dripping poisonous beast dog slobber, which burned holes as it hit the ground.

"Thank you, stable boy," said three booming dog voices and a thousand hissing snake ones.

"N-no problem," said Demon nervously, backing away slightly.

Then Cerberus raised his heads and sniffed the air.

"WOOF! WOOF! WOOF!" he bayed out of all three mouths, charging at the silver gate, which flew open as he hit it. Demon and Orpheus stared as Cerberus raced toward the plain, barking all the way. Suddenly there was a cacophony of human yells and screams, and they watched Georgios, the annoying tour guide, fling his red placard away as he took to his heels and ran as fast as he could, stomach wobbling before him.

"Serves him right," said Orpheus unsympathetically. "Humans aren't meant to come to the Underworld while they're still alive. I hope Cerberus eats him."

"I do ssso agree with you, dear Orpheusss," said a soft, sibilant voice behind them. "But it'sss not Georgiosss'sss time to die yet. My Guardian will sssimply play with him for a while, then herd him and his cussstomersss back to the upper world." Demon whirled around and fell to his knees as Hades dropped a black-gauntleted hand on his shoulder. Orpheus dissolved into a streak of mist and disappeared through the open gates with a ghostly moan of fear.

"Jussst in time, ssstable boy. Jussst in time. My ghossst dragonsss *will* be disssappointed. Are you sure you wouldn't like to give them sssome sssatisssfaction? After all, you did ssso nearly fail to cure my Guardian in time. Look at how the monssstersss almossst got out."

Demon shuddered. "N-n-no th-thank you, Y-y-your D-deathly I-illustriousness, I-I'll p-pass." Over Hades's shoulder, he could see a few of the Skeleton Guards still battling the last few monster arms. Their gray stone bones were spattered with green blood. The rest were busy filling in the cracks in the ground and throwing cut-off arms back down where they had come from. It was a gruesome sight.

Hades looked slyly at Demon. "Very well," he said. "But I must insssissst you come to a little feassst with me and my dear queen. I'm sure you're VERY hungry by now!" Demon gulped, willing his stomach not to rumble. He was STARVING, but he knew he couldn't accept the god of death's invitation. What could he say? Would Hades fry him to a crisp if he refused? There was an uncomfortable silence as Demon thought feverishly.

"There'll be ssstuffed vine leavesss and roasssted sssalmon and honey cakesss," Hades said temptingly. Demon's mouth watered. Could it really do any harm? Just one little honey cake? Just a tiny piece of salmon? He was about to open his mouth to say yes, when an invisible hand clamped over it and prevented him.

"Hello, dear Uncle Hades," said Hermes, pulling off his invisibility helmet and popping into view, giving Demon a stern shake. "Must rush. Zeus wants his stable boy back. Preferably in one piece. So kind of you to invite him to dinner, but he'll have to decline."

He seized Demon under one arm, whisked the silver box under the other, and tossed his helmet back onto his head. With a whoosh, they rose into the air and zoomed away, leaving Hades hissing and screaming with frustration and rage behind them.

"Wretched messsenger," he howled. "Jussst wait till I get my handsss on you! I WANTED that ssstable boy!"

"Lucky I was around," said Hermes. "Or you might have been in *real* trouble."

Demon let out the breath he'd been holding ever since Hermes had picked him up. His heart felt as if it were trying to crawl out from under his ribs. He imagined being stable boy to Hades and shivered. It would have been TERRIBLE.

"Thank you, Hermes," he said gratefully.

"Hey, think nothing of it," replied the god, snickering slightly. "Anything to annoy old Death Face."

Demon swallowed. "W-will Hades come after me again?" he asked.

"No no, don't worry, Pandemonius. It's me he's angry with. But I'd avoid him for a while just the same."

Demon vowed silently to do just that.

CHAPTER 10

THE STABLES AGAIN

Demon tried to look down at himself. It was a very odd experience being invisible. He could feel his body perfectly well, and he could feel Hermes's arm around his waist. He just couldn't see anything except the landscape below. He drew his legs up at the sight of the angry ghosts milling around on the banks of the Styx.

"I think we'll give old Charon a miss this time," said Hermes. "I wasn't lying when I said Zeus wants you back quickly. The Stables are starting to smell again. Aphrodite is complaining that all her nightdresses stink of poo."

"Oh no!" Demon exclaimed. "What happened? I left Doris the Hydra in charge. It was supposed to clean up and feed everyone."

"Ah!" said Hermes. "The Hydra, eh? Well, I'm sorry to tell you it's had a little problem."

Demon clutched the invisible arm holding him as they swerved around the corners of the dark tunnels. "W-what problem?" he asked, his starving stomach beginning to feel a bit queasy.

"Apparently it, uh, snacked on a bit too much ambrosia cake itself instead of giving it to the other beasts. It's been lying in its pen moaning with a bad stomachache ever since you left."

"Oh! Poor thing!" said Demon. "It's not really very smart. Maybe it misunderstood me." He hated to think of any of his beasts being in pain or discomfort. "Can Iris take us back really quickly? I need to give it something from the box."

Quite soon, he wished he hadn't asked that question. The fast version of the Iris Express was even more scary and sickening than the normal one. His whole face felt as if it were being torn off backward as they zoomed up at warp speed. He fell out onto the warm, sunbaked earth of Olympus gasping and wheezing. Hermes gently placed the box beside him.

"I've got another message to deliver," he said. "See you around!" And with that, he was gone again. The familiar smell of beast poo drifted into Demon's nostrils as he hauled himself upright and wobbled off toward the Stables, the box in his arms.

"About time, Pan's scrawny kid," said the griffin grumpily from its post beside the Hydra's pen. "I'm STARVING!"

"FOOD FOOD FOOD FOOD!" went a chorus of barks, moos, baas, squeals, squeaks, hisses, and neighs.

"ALL RIGHT!" Demon yelled. "I'll feed you as soon as I've mended Doris!" He looked at the box. "Come on," he said. "A Hydra stomachache should be easy after what we've just been through."

Ten minutes later the Hydra was sleeping contentedly, little whuffling snores coming out of its nine heads, and Demon was busy shoveling ambrosia cake and golden hay into mangers. Soon there was the sound of happy chomping. His own stomach was grumbling urgently as he went to get his wheelbarrow, brush, and shovel. Could he risk popping over to Hestia's kitchen to see if there was a spare something he could eat? No, he decided. He didn't want Aphrodite complaining again. The fewer gods and goddesses who wanted to turn him into little piles of ash, the better. He stuffed several pieces of ambrosia cake into his mouth at once and chewed them down thankfully. They didn't taste half bad after a whole day of Underworld adventures.

Demon tipped barrowload after barrowload down the poo chute, but there was a deathly hush from the hundred-armed monsters below. Maybe they were too busy regrowing the arms the Skeleton Guard had cut off, he thought, feeling a little bit sorry for them. He swept and shoveled till he was totally exhausted, only just avoiding the giant scorpion's stinger, which made him think of Orion down in the Underworld. He wondered how Orpheus was doing, too, feeling sad that they hadn't had a chance to say good-bye. When the Stables were spick-and-span again, he put all his tools away and slumped down on a bale of golden hay, feeling Helios's rays warming him through.

"Pleased to be back?" asked the griffin, coming out of the Stables and pecking him gently on the shoulder.

"SO pleased," said Demon, with an enormous yawn, snuggling up against its warm yellow body. "Home at last," he mumbled drowsily as his eyes closed.

"I wouldn't get too comfortable, stable boy," the griffin whispered in his ear. "Another Important Visitor turned up here last night."

But Demon was fast asleep and didn't hear him.

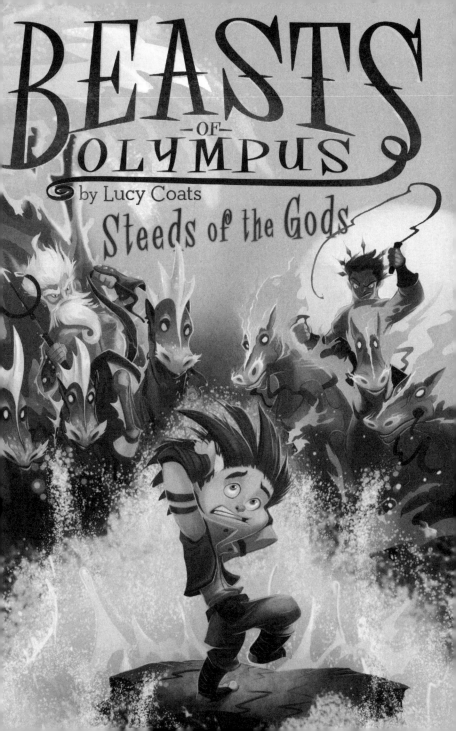

For Faith, who reads enough books
to feed a griffin

by Lucy Coats   art by Brett Bean

Steeds of the Gods

CHAPTER 1

THE GOD FROM THE SEA

Demon first found out about his latest Important Visitor when he heard Melanie the naiad shriek. He dropped his shovel in the poo barrow and rushed over to the spring outside the Stables of the Gods to see what was happening. Melanie stood shivering and curtsying at the side of her spring, her long blue hair streaming down her back. In the middle of the water stood a huge bearded figure wearing a crown of jeweled seashells. He held a large golden trident in his left hand.

"Pah!" he spat, wringing out his robes and striding up to Demon. "Freshwater. Mimsy-flimsy stuff. Give me a pool of salty sea brine any day."

Demon's heart sank into his sandals as he bowed

low. An early morning visit from a god was never good news—and this was Zeus's own brother. What could Poseidon, god of the sea, want with him at this hour?

"How can I help you, Your Watery Wondrousness?" he asked.

"Ha!" said Poseidon, bringing his hand down on Demon's shoulder so hard, the young boy fell on his backside in the dust. "Watery Wondrousness. I like it. Up you get, now, stable boy. I need to talk to you." He reached down and offered a hand wearing a glove that seemed to be made of sapphires the size and shape of barnacles. Demon took the hand cautiously. It felt cold and rather wet, and the jewel barnacles scraped his fingers, but he didn't say anything. It was best not to with gods. They took offense very easily, he'd found, and that could lead to Bad Things.

Poseidon was looking around him. The nine

green heads of Doris the Hydra were peering shyly around the Stables' door, long eyelashes fluttering. Demon could see the griffin lurking behind them.

"That the beastie you cured for Hera?" the god asked. "Looks pretty healthy to me."

"Yes, Your Serene Saltiness," said Demon. "It helps me out around the Stables now." Doris fluttered its eighteen sets of eyelashes and rattled its buckets.

"Snackies?" Doris asked hopefully. Demon ignored it. He'd only just cured its bellyache from eating too much ambrosia cake, and he wasn't risking a repeat.

"Show me around, stable boy," said Poseidon.

Demon took the god up and down the stalls. He warned him politely not to poke at the giant scorpion with the pointy end of his trident, and explained about the Cattle of the Sun not being able to eat ambrosia cake because of the terrible gas it gave them. By the time they'd almost finished, Demon was feeling a bit more optimistic. Poseidon seemed much friendlier than the scary Hera, and a lot nicer than sinister Hades. Demon shivered, remembering his recent trip down to the Underworld to save the life of Hades's great beastdog, Cerberus. He'd only just escaped being eaten by the King of Death's skeleton dragons, thanks to the help of Hermes, the gods' chief messenger. Stopping at the last pen, he gestured at the creatures within.

"These are the Ethiopian winged horses, Your Royal Godnificence," he said, patting the shiny golden horns in the middle of the boss horse's forehead. "I fly out on Keith here most days—they need a lot of exercise to keep their wings strong." Keith neighed enthusiastically.

"What do you know of Hippocamps, stable boy?" Poseidon asked abruptly. Demon racked his brain. Hippocamps? What in the name of Zeus's toenails were they?

"I-I-I've never met one, Your Outstanding Oceanosity," he said.

"No. I suppose you wouldn't have. I don't bring them up here much—no proper seawater, you see." He clapped his hands together. "You'll just have to come back to the Stables of the Ocean with me and examine them. Their scales are all falling off, and none of my sea people seem to know why." Demon gulped and turned pale. He didn't know what to do. How could he leave his own Stables again? If there was no one to clean them out and look after the beasts, the whole of Olympus would smell of poo. Then the goddesses would get furious and turn him into one big Demon-size pile of ash. Poseidon frowned, his shaggy eyebrows throwing off silvery-green sparks.

"You don't seem very happy, stable boy," he

growled. The atmosphere in the Stables had suddenly become heavy and close, as if a big thunderstorm was coming. The winged horses whinnied in alarm as gusts of wind began to whip the dust up into mini-tornadoes. Demon hurriedly forced a smile onto his face. He should have known that Poseidon's nice mood was too good to last.

"N-no, n-no, Your Awesome Aquaticness. I-I-I was just w-wondering what medicines to bring. I-I'll go and fetch my box immediately."

"Very well," said Poseidon, his frown disappearing as suddenly as it had come. "I'll go and visit with my brother Zeus. I have a small matter I need to discuss with him. Be ready when I return." With a swish and a swirl of his still-dripping cloak, he left the Stables, depositing a small pile of flapping fish and a large, angry lobster at Demon's feet. The boy leaped out of reach of the lobster's clacking claws and ran for the hospital shed. The griffin, after it had gobbled up the fish, loped after him on its lion's feet.

"Dearie me, Pan's scrawny kid," it sniggered, when it had caught up with him. "Looks like you're in trouble, whichever way you jump."

"I know," Demon panted as he ran. "What am I going to DO, Griffin? I can't just leave all of you on your own again. Look what happened with Doris last time. And what do I do if he keeps me down there for ages? Aphrodite will probably turn me into a pile of burnt rose petals if her nighties start to smell of poo again."

"We-e-e-ll," said the griffin slowly, "I suppose the Nemean Lion and I could make sure Doris cleans out the stables and doesn't eat all the ambrosia cake again. Lion's been a bit depressed since you gave it that fluffy green skin. It'll cheer it up no end to have a job to do."

"Would you really?" asked Demon as he skidded

to a halt in front of the hospital shed. "I don't think it'll take very long. I'll be back in a day or so, I swear." The griffin looked at him slyly out of the corner of its orange eye.

"If you'll promise to give me meat at least once a week when you get back," it said. "Otherwise the deal's off." Demon groaned. Meat was really hard to come by on Olympus, unless it was a feast day. But he didn't really have a choice. He'd think about how to get around the griffin's request when he got back. If Poseidon hadn't turned him into a Demon-shaped coral reef by then, of course.

"All RIGHT!" he said crossly. "But you have to do the job properly. I don't want to find a piece of hay out of place or a single speck of dust in any of the stalls. And I especially don't want to find Doris sick again. Understand?"

"Trust me, Pan's scrawny kid," it said, giving Demon a sideways orange wink that made it look most UNtrustworthy. Then it flapped its eagle wings once and soared up to sit on the rooftop. "Better hurry up," it called down. "I see old Fishface coming out of Zeus's palace. He doesn't look in a very good mood."

Demon's magical medicine box didn't turn out to be in a very good mood, either, when he told it they were going to Poseidon's realm. He could hear it grumbling behind him as it waddled its way toward the Stables on its short, stumpy legs.

"Shut up, box," Demon hissed as he saw Poseidon in the distance. "You'll get us into trouble."

"Implementing aquasynchrous marine interface," it muttered. "As for you, I hope you get Error Code 7533 and turn into a sea cucumber." It withdrew its legs and thumped down beside him, ejecting a kind of see-through skin from its sides, which spread over its whole surface, sealing it completely. Demon stared at it. How was he supposed to open it now? But he had no time to think about that, because Poseidon was stomping toward him, muttering to himself. The air became thick and still again, and there was a strong smell of ozone.

"Come with me, stable boy," the god said, gripping Demon's arm with his barnacle-gloved hand and, without another word, pulling him toward Melanie's spring. Demon grabbed onto the box's now-slightly-sticky-feeling handle and tugged. Slipping and sliding, it bounced behind him as he was dragged into the pool, sinking rapidly downward before he could take more than one panicked, gasping breath of air.

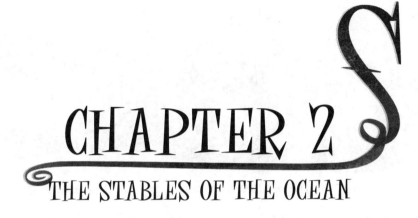

CHAPTER 2

THE STABLES OF THE OCEAN

Demon held his breath for as long as he could, but eventually long streamers of silvery bubbles began to gush out of his mouth. He kicked and struggled against the god's hold as he took in a big breath of seawater. Choking, his vision began to go black at the edges. *I'm going to drown*, he thought. Just then, Poseidon turned to look at him, godly green eyes flashing as they took in what was happening. Whirling his trident around in one swift movement, he pointed it at Demon. Bright purple streaks shot

out of its three golden tips and weaved themselves swiftly into a net that dropped over Demon's head and body. It encased him completely before it sank into his skin and disappeared.

"Yurrch! Yech! Yuck!" he wheezed, hacking up seawater and snot from the bottom of his lungs. Offy and Yukus, the two snakes that made up his magical healing necklace, curled and uncurled themselves anxiously around his neck. Demon just hoped they weren't going to get any ideas about plunging down his throat to suck the rest of the water out.

"You weedy earthbound half-mortals," said

Poseidon as they started to zoom downward
through the dark water again. "No stamina, that's
your trouble. You'll be all right now that I've given
you some of my sea power."

Just as Demon was getting used to the strange
sensation of breathing water as if it were air, his
heart gave a panicky thump. With all the coughing
and drowning, he'd somehow let go of his magic
healing box. He craned desperately over one
shoulder. A flash of silver caught his eye, just as
he felt a bump at the back of his knees. The box
had developed silvery fins and was swimming
clumsily at his heels. He closed his eyes in relief.

Annoying as it was, there was no way he was going to cure a Hippocamp without its help. Whatever a Hippocamp was.

"Follow me, stable boy," said Poseidon as they landed on the ocean floor. He swam off toward a rocky mountain covered in silver seaweed, with Demon dog-paddling awkwardly behind him. He wasn't used to swimming so fast, and rather wished he could grow fins like the box had. Quite soon he saw a wash of blue-green light in front of him. Two enormous golden doors stood open at the entrance to the mountain. They were guarded by two brawny creatures, half man, half fish, who thumped their spears on the ground and snapped to rigid, tail-quivering attention as Poseidon stalked past. Demon and the box hurried along at his side.

"All hail the Father of Oceans! All hail the King of the Seas," they shouted out in a dreary monotone, making Demon jump.

"Yes, yes," said Poseidon testily. "No need for all that." He bent his head down toward Demon. "My guards, the Tritons, have loyal hearts but few brains. Now, come on, stable boy. My poor Hippocamps won't get any better if you just stand there gaping." Demon began to hear a rustling, scraping sort of sound, and as they turned a rocky corner, he saw a series of nine stalls made from what looked like multicolored coral. Every stall was filled with a very odd-looking beast. Each had a shiny, smooth-skinned white horse head and chest, and front legs that ended in dinner plate–size hooves surrounded by a ruff of spiny fins. Their backs and hindquarters were like monstrous fish, and their long, golden, spike-finned manes waved in the watery current. Demon could see the problem immediately. The round greenish-bronze scales that covered their rear ends were ragged and torn. Each Hippocamp had big, pink, raw-looking patches where there were no scales at all.

"Oh! You poor things," said Demon, walking over to pat the nearest one, which promptly reared, squealed with rage, and bared its large square teeth at him. "Stop that," he said in his firmest beast-taming voice. "I'm here to help you."

"Make them comfortable, stable boy," ordered Poseidon. "Find out what's wrong and fix it. You may ask one of the Tritons to bring you up to the throne room when you're finished. I have a meeting with Helios to go to now." He paused, frowning, as a cloud of tiny golden fish zipped in and out of his beard. "Can't think what my wretched sky cousin wants with me. Fire and water don't mix, you know." With that, he launched himself upward and shot through a hole in the ceiling. Demon sighed. Although the sea god hadn't threatened to turn him into a pile of burnt seaweed, nobody needed to tell him that things wouldn't go well for him if he didn't find a cure for the Hippocamps.

"Right, box," he said, turning around. "We have work to do. Let's find out what's wrong with these poor beasts." But the box had disappeared. "Box!" he said again, peering into the dark corners of the Stables of the Ocean. "Box! Stop sulking and come here at once." There was no reply. Trying not to panic, Demon looked into every stall and checked behind every rock. Then he swam back down the passage to the golden doors. "Have you seen my silver box?" he asked the Tritons. They shook their heads. Demon wanted to kick something. He wished he'd never taken on this stupid job. He was swimming back toward the Stables of the Ocean, thinking gloomy thoughts about all the horrible things Poseidon was going to do to him now, when he heard a shout behind him.

"Lost something?" asked a high little voice. Paddling around clumsily, he saw a girl in a blue floaty robe. She had two braids of long dark-green hair wound around her head, firmly clipped in place by several pairs of golden crabs; very pale green skin; and legs that ended in two neat flipper feet. In her arms she was holding a struggling silver box, and her mischievous grin showed a mouthful of small pearly teeth.

"Oh, thank goodness!" he said. "Where did you find it?"

"Well," she replied, blushing a deeper shade of green, "I saw a big silver box lying about doing nothing. And then I thought the queen might like it for keeping her spare crowns in. So I kind of stole it. Only . . . only then it sort of came alive and told me I'd be in trouble with Poseidon if I didn't bring it back here. So I thought I'd better do what it said. I don't want to be turned into a sea monster! He did that to one of my cousins, and now he's a giant ugly whale thing."

"Just as well," said Demon, a
double surge of anger and relief
shooting through him.

"If I'd lost it, you wouldn't have been the only one Poseidon turned into something horrible." He swam forward and grabbed the box, giving it a little pat of thanks before heading back toward the Hippocamps. The girl followed him.

"What are you doing?" she asked.

"Trying to cure Poseidon's Hippocamps, of course," he said, rather carefully approaching the horse who'd tried to bite him. "Can't you see their scales are all falling off? Now go away. I'm a bit busy, in case you hadn't noticed." The girl didn't move.

"I know the magic Hippocamp trick," she said, watching thoughtfully as the Hippocamp bared its teeth again and laid back its smooth green-bronze ears. "If you're interested." Faster than Zeus's lightning, the horse snaked out its head and clamped its jaws around Demon's arm, its blue eyes rolling.

"Aarrghh!" he yelled, jumping backward and leaving a large chunk of his flesh behind. Immediately, Offy and Yukus slithered off his neck and twined themselves around the wound, sealing and healing it. He turned to look at her. "What magic Hippocamp trick?" he asked, his voice full of suspicion. He wasn't going to trust someone who'd admitted to stealing his magic box *that* easily.

"This," she replied, gliding over to the Hippocamp and seizing it by the nostrils. She brought its head close to her face and blew a stream of bubbles up its nose. At once, its eyelids drooped, and it went all dopey. Demon was impressed in spite of himself. It was as good as his father's magical Pan pipes. The girl turned toward him, a slightly smug look on her face.

"You can examine him properly now. He'll stay calm for a while. I'm Eunice, by the way, daughter of Nereus, and one of the Nereids."

"I'm Demon," he said, holding out a hand. "Official stable boy to the gods on Olympus, and son of Pan. Nice to meet you."

Eunice giggled, holding out her own webbed hand. "We don't do that down here—we wiggle ours instead. But it's nice to meet you, too, Demon. And even nicer that you're not one of my forty-nine stupid sisters. I'm so bored of their fancy jewelry-trying-on parties and silly gossip. I want to do something interesting. I wish I could have a proper job like you—I'd love to look after the Hippocamps. I'd be better at it than those stupid Tritons, anyway!"

"Well, I guess you can help me with this lot, then," Demon said. "But we'd better hurry. I don't want to find out what Poseidon will do if I don't report back to him soon." He turned to the silver box. "I need a cure for these Hippocamps, please." The box began to flash blue as it flapped its fins and moved closer to the still-dopey beast. The see-through skin around the box bulged slightly, and a tube with a suction cup emerged from under the barely open lid, moving over the ragged, peeling scales with a slurping sound before sliding back inside.

"What IS that thing?" asked Eunice, her pale aquamarine eyes widening as she watched.

"Hephaestus made it for me. You know, the smith god? The one who makes all the magic armor for the Olympians? He's really good at inventing stuff." He was about to explain what the box did, when it started to flash and make whirring noises. "Here it goes. We'll have a cure in a minute," he said, crossing his fingers.

"Running preliminary diagnostics," said the box, its tinny tones muffled in the water.

"What's 'preliminary diagnostics'?" Eunice asked.

"Take no notice," said Demon. "It uses fancy terms to make it sound clever, but mostly because it likes to annoy me. 'Diagnostics' just means it's looking for the right medicine." The box spat a blue spark and made what sounded suspiciously like a snort.

"Hipponautikos akropyodermatitis detected in subject," it said. Demon glared at it. "More commonly known as persistent itchy itch."

"Itchy," the Hippocamp whinnied drowsily. Then its eyes snapped open. "ITCHY!" it screamed. "ITCHYitchyITCHYitchyITCHY!" Then it flung itself backward, writhing and wriggling its scales against the pen walls. Immediately, its stablemates joined in, until the whole cave was filled with an echoing chorus of horrible Hippocamp screams and the harsh sound of scales being rubbed off against coral.

CHAPTER 3

A GODLY FIGHT

"STOP IT!" yelled Demon. But it was no good. The Hippocamps were in a dreadful frenzy of agonizing itchiness. Neither he nor Eunice could get anywhere near them to blow soothing bubbles up their noses—there were too many flailing fish tails and razor-sharp hooves flying about to even try. Demon fumbled inside the front of his tunic and pulled out his dad's magic pipes, hoping against hope that they'd work underwater. Cramming them against his lips, he blew hard. A swirl of silver music curled out, quite visible against the churning turbulence around the terrified sea beasts. The music split into nine parts and shot forward, coiling around each Hippocamp's muzzle like a halter. There was an immediate silence. Every one of the nine panicked creatures sighed deeply, closed its blue eyes, and fell asleep.

"Wow!" said Eunice. "That's way cooler than *my* trick!"

Demon didn't waste a moment.

"Quick, box," he said, "I need a cure right now, before they all wake up again." For once the box didn't argue. The shiny membrane that covered it strained and swelled, and a large copper-colored pot of ointment erupted from its lid with a loud *POP*.

"Apply liberally to all areas," said the box. Then, with a wheezing sound, it closed and shut down. Demon grabbed the pot and wrenched at the lid. It wouldn't budge.

"Come on," he said. "Come ON! Open, you Zeus-blasted thing!"

"Here," said Eunice, swimming forward to help him. "I'll hold, you twist." Demon strained and grunted, and at last, with an earsplitting *CLUNK*, the top came off. As soon as the pot was open, they dug their hands into the gloopy yellow gunk inside and started to smear it over the Hippocamps' scales.

"I really hope this works," said Demon, "because I never want to hear those Hippocamps screaming again. It was AWFUL."

"I know," Eunice agreed, wiping the last of the ointment off her fingers. Just then, the first of the Hippocamps gave a sleepy whinny. Demon crossed his fingers and toes. Could the ointment have worked so soon? Maybe the Hippocamps would be hungry when they woke up. He looked around him, noticing several bales of silver seaweed piled up in one corner.

"Is that what they eat?" he asked, pointing. Eunice nodded. "Well, at least it's not leftover ambrosia cake," he said. "That would get disgustingly soggy down here." As they swam around, filling each manger, Eunice shot a barrage of questions at him about the Stables of the Gods and Olympus. How many beasts did he have to look after? (A lot.) Why didn't he like ambrosia cake? (Because it was boring eating it day after day, and it didn't taste that nice!) What was the most difficult thing he'd ever had to cure? (Doris the Hydra's cut-off heads.) He hadn't talked so much in ages, and he found he liked being with someone his own age a lot.

"Eunice . . . ," he started. But then all the

Hippocamps woke up at once, plunged their noses into the full mangers, and started munching.

"Look!" she squealed. "They're getting better!" Demon looked. Their scales were gleaming and healthy once more, with tiny new goldy-bronze ones starting to fill in the now-healed pink patches.

"Oh! Thank Zeus's left armpit," he said. Demon glanced down. "Oh, all right. Thank you, too, box." The box glowed a pleased kind of blue and flapped its fins. "Now come on, we'd better go and find one of those Tritons to take us to Poseidon."

Eunice rolled her eyes. "Stupid Tritons. I bet the Hippocamps got sick because those idiots weren't looking after them properly. It wouldn't have happened if I'd been in charge. Don't worry—I'll take you to the throne room. I'd better join my stupid sisters again, anyway, or I'll be in trouble, and that's where they'll be." Chattering on, she led the way upward through the hole in the cave ceiling. Demon followed, trying to copy the graceful, easy way she swam without much success. As he floundered at her heels, he sort of wished Poseidon had given him flippers as well as underwater breathing.

He was concentrating so hard on his swimming that he didn't notice when Eunice stopped dead in front of him.

"*OOF!*" she gasped as he rammed right into her back, knocking her head over heels through an arched doorway and into a gleaming pool of air and light. Demon suddenly noticed that the water had gotten very hot around him just as Eunice seized him by the hand and dragged him behind a pillar.

"Shh!" she hissed fiercely. "Look!" Demon took a choking breath of damp air and looked about him with wide, awed eyes. He saw a glittering cavern with an endlessly high deep-blue arched ceiling that was decorated with sparkling diamonds to imitate the night sky above the ocean. The smooth walls glowed the exact shade of the inside of a pearly oyster shell. There was a small crowd of sea people and dolphins pressed up against the walls, all looking terrified. In the very center of the room was a high dais with a throne placed on it that seemed to be carved out of one giant sapphire. In front of the throne stood two gods, nose to nose and clearly very angry.

"Say that again!" roared Poseidon, his beard bristling as the water roiled and bubbled around his feet.

"My celestial horses can beat your slow old Hippocamps any day of the week," yelled a purple-robed god who Demon knew must be Helios because of the golden crown of sun rays on his head. Beams of heat shot out from his eyes, turning the light in the cavern orangey-yellow and the water even hotter.

"Gentlegods, gentlegods, there's only one way to settle this," said a voice, apparently coming from nowhere, a voice Demon knew very well. The god Hermes took off his invisibility hat and strolled out of thin air toward the furious gods of sea and sun. "You two must challenge each other to a race. I suggest once around the earth, one of you taking the sea route and the other going by sky. Invite all the gods and goddesses to watch—and the victor gives a feast." The water calmed and became cooler.

"Very well," said Poseidon, stalking back to his throne and sitting down. "Consider the challenge given, Sun Boy."

"Done," said Helios. "I'll meet you seven days from now, Father of Fishiness. Prepare to lose that golden trident of yours!" With that, he let out a blast of blinding light and disappeared.

"Wretched jumped-up Titan," muttered Poseidon,

his eyebrows twitching into a fierce frown. "Always trying to pick a fight." The water in the throne room darkened and began to churn. Several sea nymphs and mermaids squeaked and fled.

"Come on, dear uncle," said Hermes soothingly. "I've seen those Hippocamps of yours. They're fast, and if you rest them well, they should beat Helios easily. Don't forget, those celestial horses of his will be pulling the sun behind them—they won't exactly be fresh."

"Hmm," said Poseidon. "Well, my Hippocamps aren't exactly in top form, either. At least they *weren't*. Maybe Zeus's stable boy has managed to cure them. Where is the wretched brat, anyway? He should have reported in by now." Eunice gave Demon a little shove.

"Go on," she whispered. "Tell him the good news. It might put him in a better temper." Demon swam clumsily forward.

"Er, I'm here, Your Opulent Oceanosity," he said as Hermes winked at him encouragingly. "The Hippocamps are doing well. Their scales are growing back nicely, and they're eating like . . . well . . . horses."

Poseidon scowled at him. "They'd better be fine," he growled, "or I'll have you on your knees scrubbing salt off of seaweed for the next hundred years. Consider yourself assigned to the Stables of the Ocean till further notice. I want my Hippocamps in tip-top condition for the race. You're looking after them full-time till then."

Demon's heart gave a horrible blip and sank right down to his toes. What sort of state would his own Stables be in after a whole week? He'd sworn to the griffin that he'd be back in a couple of days—he didn't trust it and the Nemean Lion to cope for any longer than that, anyway. What WAS he going to do? Giving Hermes a look of complete desperation, he bowed to Poseidon and stammered out the only thing he thought might stop the god from turning him into a coral reef.

"Y-yes, Y-your M-mighty G-godnificence, I'll get down there and see to it at once."

CHAPTER 4

HERMES TO THE RESCUE

"Please, Hermes, please," Demon begged the messenger god silently as he swam slowly back toward where he'd left Eunice. *"I really, really need to talk to you."* But Hermes stayed firmly in the middle of the throne room, chatting away with Poseidon in his usual lighthearted manner. The water was calm and cool again, and he could hear chattering voices ahead of him and squeals of girlish laughter.

"Ooh! Here he is!"

"Isn't he cute?"

"Why don't you introduce us to your *boyfriend*, Eunice?"

Suddenly he was surrounded by a whole gaggle of Nereid girls, each dressed in a different-colored floaty robe. It was like being in the middle of a whole garden of sea flowers. Demon felt himself blushing as Eunice took him firmly by the arm.

"Girls, this is Demon. Demon, these are my sisters, Maira, Neso, Erato, Halia . . ." She stopped. "Oh, never mind. You'll never remember all forty-nine of them, and they're too silly to bother with, anyway." She pulled him out of the circle of admiring glances and giggles, and turned to face them. "Now go away. I've got to show Demon the way back to the stables." Pouting, the pack of girls swam away.

One of them turned back, shaking her finger at Eunice. "Just wait till I tell Amphitrite about you,

Eunice. She'll be cross if you're not there to brush her hair at bedtime. You're meant to be nymph-in-waiting to the queen, not helping some stupid stable boy."

"I don't care, Thetis," said Eunice defiantly. "You know I like being with sea beasts more than brushing royal hair. And he's not stupid. Come on, Demon, let's go." By this time, Demon's face was redder than a ripe cherry. Why did girls always have to be so giggly and weird? Why couldn't they just act normal? He wrenched his arm out of Eunice's grip.

"I'll be fine," he said, horribly embarrassed. "You don't need to come. I can manage to find my own way." Eunice's face fell.

"Oh. All right, then. I just thought . . ." She looked so downcast that Demon immediately felt guilty.

"I didn't mean . . ."

"I only . . . ," they said together.

"You go first," said Eunice, still looking upset.

Demon could see he needed to explain.

"I didn't mean to hurt your feelings," he said. "It's just . . . your sisters . . . Queen Amphitrite . . . I don't want to get you in trouble . . ." He was suddenly not sure what to say.

"Really? Is that all? Oh, never mind them. I told you they were silly, remember? And Queen Amphitrite will let me off, if I explain." Her face turned a deeper green, and Demon realized she was blushing, too. "I-I-I thought it might be because you didn't like me. My sisters always say I'm much too bossy for my own good, but I was only trying to help. I'd really like to be friends with you, if you'll let me." Demon breathed a sigh of relief. "Friends" was just fine by him, and he could definitely use all the help he could get.

"Friends," he agreed, holding out his hand and waggling it at her. "Is this how you do it?"

Eunice laughed. "Pretty much," she said,

flapping her webbed one in return.

The Hippocamps had eaten all their silver seaweed by the time their new friends got down to the Stables of the Ocean. Just then, Demon heard a loud whistle, and Hermes dropped through the hole in the ceiling.

"Fancy seeing you here, stable boy," said the god, his usual mischievous grin spread all over his face. "Did a little fishy whisper that you might be needing me? Are you in trouble AGAIN?"

"Yes," said Demon, too relieved to see him to bother with politeness. "Or I *will* be if I leave the Stables of the Gods with Griffin and Lion in charge for too much longer—and Poseidon wants me to stay here for a whole week. You know what happened the last time."

"I do, indeed. And we can't have the whole of Olympus smelling of poo again, or the goddesses will be after you." Hermes tapped one long fingernail against his very white teeth, clearly thinking. "Tell you what. I have a young man called Autolykos who's in a bit of trouble at the moment over some cattle he stole. He's not bad with beasts, and he owes me a favor or two. I expect he'd look after the Stables for a week. He's a cunning little fellow."

Demon tried to picture a clever thief looking after the giant scorpion, and failed miserably. But what other choice did he have? "Thank you, Hermes," he said gratefully. Then he had an awful thought. What if this Autolykos got badly bitten or even stung by the giant scorpion? He'd need protection. Demon put a hand to his neck and unfastened his magical snake necklace. "Maybe I'd better lend him Offy and Yukus. Otherwise he might get killed. Some of my beasts aren't very friendly, you know. And what about Hephaestus's box?"

"No, no," said Hermes. "You keep all that. I'll make sure he's safe, don't worry. You just get on with looking after these fine beasties. I've got places to be, people to see. Bye for now!" With a wave of his hand, the god put on his invisibility hat and vanished.

"Was that really Hermes?" Eunice whispered. "Only . . . only he doesn't seem like a g—I mean . . ." Her voice stuttered to a halt, but Demon knew exactly what she'd been trying to say.

"Doesn't seem like a god?" he asked. She nodded. "Well, no, he doesn't. At least not like some of the other ones I've met. I'm always scared they're going to turn me into little piles of ash—apart from Heffy and Hestia—but Hermes is really ni—"

Before he could finish his sentence, Eunice, cowering with fear, had darted into a cleft in the rock. A second later he saw why. With a rush of dark water, Poseidon swam into the cave. Demon fell to his knees beside the silver box.

"H-h-hello, Your Serene Saltiness," he said. Poseidon gestured impatiently.

"Get up, get up. All this wretched bowing and scraping drives me mad. Now, let me see how my lovely Hippocamps are doing." Crooning in a most un-king-like way, he went from stall to stall, patting noses and stroking spiky manes. "Well, well. They seem quite recovered." He clapped Demon on the shoulder, sending him shooting backward through the water. "Good job, stable boy. You deserve a reward. Now, let's harness them up and put them through their paces. I'll show you why I'm going to win this race."

Poseidon showed Demon where his racing chariot was, and how to harness the nine Hippocamps to it. Meanwhile, Eunice remained huddled in her rocky hideaway, putting a green finger to her lips. Demon tried not to look at her, not wanting to give her away, as he and the sea god fastened buckles and threaded straps together. Poseidon's help was a big surprise. Hades had made Demon do all the hard work of harnessing the earth dragons, but the king of the sea seemed to like doing it himself. Finally, the chariot was ready.

"In you get," said the sea god, pointing to the seat beside him. Demon climbed in rather nervously. The last chariot he'd been in was Hera's, and that hadn't been a good experience at all. This one was a bit different. It was made in the shape of a long streamlined silver shell, and had two low bucket seats lined with cushions of soft, spongy red sea moss. Poseidon was strapping himself into one with two thick strands of green ribbon kelp, which passed around his shoulders and clipped with two large silver crabs to a third that went between his legs. "Buckle up, stable boy," he barked. "And prepare for the ride of your life."

Scrambling into the second seat beside the king, Demon had just managed to figure out how the kelp harness fitted together when Poseidon swung his trident like a whip, and a jet of blue fire snaked out and cracked over the Hippocamps' heads. With a joyful whinny, they were off. Demon just caught a glimpse of Eunice's scared eyes flashing past before he was jolted back in his seat. He clung to his kelp straps with both hands. The Hippocamps rushed through the golden doors and past the Triton guards, and then Poseidon cracked his trident again.

"Yee-haw, giddyup," he yelled happily, his hair streaming out behind him like weeds. The Hippocamps went even faster, till all Demon could see of the underwater world rushing past him was a series of blurred streaks. Up and up and up they went. Then, with a gasp, Demon was breathing air

again. They were skimming across the top of a calm deep-blue ocean, and the Hippocamps' long, spiky manes flew like golden foam in the breeze.

CHAPTER 5

THE HORSES OF THE SUN

Demon never did manage to catch his breath properly on that wild, amazing ride. Poseidon urged his steeds to go faster and faster. By the time they sank beneath the waves again, Demon's hands were so cramped and uncomfortable from hanging on to his straps that he thought they might never unclench. The sea god looked at him sideways as he slowed the Hippocamps down and guided them gently back into the Stables of the Ocean.

"So, stable boy. How was that for you?"

Demon grinned at the god before he could stop himself. It HAD been very exciting, as well as totally terrifying! "Er, stupendous, Your Serene Saltiness. I think you're going to win. They're really quick, aren't they?"

"Quicker than anything in sea, sky, or earth, and don't you forget it. Now unharness them, and then give them a good rubdown with a sea sponge. Afterward, polish up their scales with some sea-slug slime. They'll need as much seaweed as they can eat. Later we'll take them over to my other palace at Macris. That's where the race is going to start. Got it?" Demon nodded as Poseidon shot up through the hole in the ceiling.

"Yes, Your Mighty Marineness," he said to the god's disappearing toes. Once he was sure he was alone, he peered around him. "Eunice!" he hissed. "Eunice, where are you? You can come out now." But there was no reply. Eunice was gone, and he had no idea where to find her—or any of the items Poseidon had mentioned. There wasn't a sea sponge to be seen anywhere, let alone any sea-slug slime. He led each Hippocamp back to its pen and hung the harnesses up. Pushing the racing chariot back to the small cave it had come from, he wondered what he was going to do. Then he looked at the Hippocamp who'd bitten him, and had an idea.

"Could you tell me where the stable supplies are, please?" he asked politely. But the Hippocamp just rolled its blue eyes at him menacingly and let out a loud whinny.

"Sponge," it neighed. "Slime. Seaweed." Then the whole lot of them started.

"SPONGE. SLIME. SEAWEED," they chorused. They might be fast, Demon thought, but they hadn't so much as a brain cell among them.

"All right, all right! I'll find them myself," he shouted above the noise. But search as he might, he couldn't find anything but the seaweed. With a tired sigh, he tipped it into the mangers to shut the Hippocamps up. He then sat down on a coral ledge next to the silver box.

"Don't suppose you've seen any of that stuff Poseidon mentioned, have you, box?" The box didn't answer, but a beam of blue shot out from its lid, lighting up the murky water in the darkest corner of the stables. Demon saw what looked like a cupboard door in the rocky wall. It had a tiny knob in the shape of a starfish. Wrenching it open, he discovered everything he needed inside.

Armed with sponges, he rubbed down each Hippocamp in turn, using Eunice's clever trick of blowing up the nostrils of any of them who looked like they might nip him. Then he turned to the big pot of sea-slug slime. It was thick and green and gloopy, and if he wasn't careful putting it on the sponge, great globs of it floated off and stuck to his tunic. He was just glad he couldn't smell it, because it looked absolutely revolting. The Hippocamps' scales were fully grown back now, and by the time he'd finished with them, they looked shiny and beautiful, and he was utterly exhausted. It had been a very long day, and he'd had nothing to eat. Curling up on some seaweed in a corner, and trying not to think about his starving stomach, Demon fell fast asleep.

He was woken by a gentle nudge on the shoulder.

"Go 'way, Griffin," he groaned, still half asleep and forgetting where he was. There was another, slightly less gentle nudge to his ribs. Demon's eyes snapped open. There in front of him was a creature with kind eyes and a mouth half open in a friendly grin. It had six starry points of light all along its body, making the whole cavern shine with a warm glow, and it was the most beautiful thing Demon had ever seen.

"Up you get, son of Pan," it said. "Queen Amphitrite wants to see you. Hop on and I'll take you to her." It gestured with a fin to its back. Demon rubbed his sleepy eyes and yawned, wondering what the queen wanted with him, and what this creature was.

"All right," he said. "But I'd better feed this lot first. I don't want Poseidon getting angry with me."

"Wise decision," said the creature. "But hurry up. You don't want to keep the queen waiting, either!" Demon hurried to fill the mangers yet again, then clambered up onto the long, smooth back, hanging on to the big curved fin.

"Er, who are you, if you don't mind me asking?" he said as they swam upward, the powerful body twisting and turning under him, making the lights within it flash and flicker like jewels.

"I'm Delphinus," it said. "Messenger dolphin to the queen. Now hang on and keep your head down. I'm taking us up by the shortcut." Demon ducked low as the dolphin raced this way and that. It moved through narrow tunnels and passageways, eventually shooting out into a brightly lit room. Shafts of sunlight poured in through long, high windows and reflected off a pool of still water, turning it golden. Demon gasped and spluttered as he breathed a sudden rush of real air again. It felt cold and clean and fresh in his lungs.

In the middle of the pool was a large island covered in soft green moss. Demon's heart sank into his sandals as he saw a crowd of brightly colored robes and recognized Eunice's giggling sisters. Reclining on a low couch among them was Queen Amphitrite, with Eunice behind her, brushing out one side of the queen's long dark-blue hair, while her sister Nereid braided tiny jeweled sea anemones into the other.

"Ouch!" cried the queen crossly. "Why do you always have to pull my hair so, Eunice?"

"Here he is, Your Majesty," said Delphinus, giving a wriggle so that Demon tipped off its back and splashed into the golden pool. Amphitrite pointed to a low stool beside her with one webbed finger.

"Swim over and sit there," she said, her voice now low and husky, like tiny pebbles washing against the shore. As Demon clambered out of the water and tried to wring the water out of his tunic, his tummy rumbled loudly. "Are you hungry, son of Pan?"

Demon nodded eagerly. He was hungrier than a starving starfish. "Yes, Your Majesty," he said, trying not to drool too obviously. Amphitrite smiled at him as Delphinus swam off again.

"Halia, fetch our guest something to eat and drink." One of the Nereids went over to a small table, then brought Demon a cup of green juice and a platter piled high with delicious-looking morsels.

"Here you are, Demon," she said, fluttering her long green eyelashes at him in a rather worrying way. Demon was too hungry to care, though. He concentrated on not stuffing everything into his mouth at once instead. He wasn't too sure how goddesses felt about table manners. If Amphitrite was anything like his mom, it was probably best not to gobble like a wild beast.

"I want to know all the gossip from Olympus," said Amphitrite, when he'd cleaned his plate for the third time. "Who's annoyed Hera lately? Is it true

about Eos's poor husband? Did Apollo really give
that stupid Midas an ass's ears?"

Demon's heart sank into his sloshy sandals. "I . . .

I don't really hear much gossip in the Stables, Your Briny Bountifulness," he said. "Well, only what Althea, Melanie, and Melia say about . . . w-w-well . . ." He stuttered into silence, but Amphitrite just waved a pale-blue webbed hand at him. Her jeweled fingernails flashed in the reflected sunlight.

"Tell me all!" she purred.

"Yes, do," sighed Eunice's sisters, sinking down at the sea queen's feet, like a shower of colorful petals, and gazing up at him expectantly. Blushing, he looked desperately at Eunice for help. She just grinned at him, shrugged, and kept on brushing her royal mistress's hair.

A long and very uncomfortable time later, Amphitrite had wrung out every morsel of information Demon had about the doings of the gods and goddesses on Olympus. She yawned and stretched like a satisfied cat. A loud hooting sounded somewhere outside, making

Demon jump nervously. He was about to ask what it was when he heard a pair of familiar-sounding voices shouting.

"Make way for the Father of Oceans, make way for the King of the Seas," bellowed the Tritons, their monotonous tones ringing around the chamber as they flung open the double doors. Amphitrite rose from her couch, glossy blue hair tumbling down her back like a shiny waterfall. She curtsied and held out a hand to Poseidon.

"Welcome, my king," she said, smiling at her husband.

"Nearly ready to go, my dear?" he asked, striding across the top of the pool toward her, his golden trident strapped across his back. Then his eyes fell on Demon, kneeling at the queen's feet. He frowned, and the room grew darker. Small wavelets began to run around the pool, slapping against the moss. "What's that stable boy doing in your chambers?" he boomed, staring at Demon suspiciously. "He's meant to be looking after my Hippocamps, not lounging about up here!"

"Don't be cross, my cockleshell," said Amphitrite, putting a hand on his arm. "I asked him up here. You know how I get about having the very latest news from Olympus."

"Very well," said Poseidon. "But I want him back now. There's a lot of packing up for him to do before we leave for Macris." He frowned again, but less ferociously. "Off you go, now, boy. I'll send one of the Tritons with you to help." Demon felt a sharp elbow prod his side, and turned to see Eunice glaring at him pointedly. He knew exactly what she wanted him to say before she even mouthed "I want to come" at him.

"Er, Your M-majesties," he said bravely, taking a deep breath and blurting it all out in a rush. "W-would it be all right if I had my friend Eunice as my helper? She's . . . she's very good with the

Hippocamps." Poseidon let out a sudden lightning crack of laughter.

"Good with the Hippocamps, is she, stable boy?" He peered down at Eunice, who was half hiding behind Demon. "Ah! Young Eunice! Aren't you the one my Tritons complain is always hanging about the stables?" Eunice nodded, looking scared. "Well, never mind that . . . You can have her, if my queen agrees . . ." He raised one bushy eyebrow at Amphitrite.

"Oh, very well," she said. "She's already tugged my hair around enough for today. But if there's even a trace of Hippocamp slime anywhere near my best hairbrush tonight, I shall turn you both into a pair of purple clown fish. Now, be off with you."

"Yes, Your Majesty," said Eunice. "I mean, no, Your Majesty. Er . . . I mean, I promise there won't be . . ." Then she curtsied hurriedly, turned, and fled. Demon was close behind her.

CHAPTER 6

THE PALACE OF MACRIS

There was a frantic bustle of activity as Eunice and Demon darted around and dodged gigantic octopus servants holding boxes and baskets. A flurry of sea people rushed this way and that, shouting orders and generally getting in one another's way.

When they reached the stables, the Hippocamps were in a high state of excitement. They neighed loudly and reared as Demon and Eunice ran about packing harnesses, grooming equipment, and bales of silvery seaweed. They used kelp ropes to tie it all onto several long, low sleds that had been left out for them. It took hours and hours. Just as Demon was tying down his silver box (which was shouting loudly that it could perfectly well swim by itself) onto the last sled, several mermen swam in. They led strange long-nosed fish beasts that grinned at them with mouths full of sharp white teeth. Their red backs were covered in arrow-like spines, and huge undulating tails swished the water around their pale, gleaming bellies.

"Ready?" asked one of the mermen in a deep, gruff voice. Demon nodded, backing warily away as the mermen wrangled kelp harnesses around the huge front fins.

"What are *those*?" he whispered.

"Oh, just some of the smaller whale monsters," Eunice said. "They're very friendly, really—as long as you don't feed them oysters. That makes them a bit crazy. My sister Keto is supposed to be in charge of them, but she's so lazy, she lets the mermen do most of the work." She looked over at him as the last sleds floated out of the stables, muffled protests from the silver box still drifting back toward them. "Thanks for letting me come with you. I just wish Poseidon would let me—" She broke off suddenly as Poseidon himself appeared in a swirl of sea foam, and by the time Demon had finished harnessing the Hippocamps to the chariot, Eunice had disappeared again. Maybe he should say something to the sea god about her looking after the Hippocamps. But he had no more time to think about it as the Hippocamps drew them swiftly over the waves to the sea god's earthly home.

Poseidon's above-water palace was a pleasant surprise. Once Poseidon had given him his instructions on how he wanted the Hippocamps fed and exercised for the next few days, Demon started to settle them down in their new homes.

The stables were in a light, airy cave, with spacious stalls where the Hippocamps could splash about to their hearts' content, and with places to store everything else. There was even a tiny alcove above, with a small sleeping pallet and a blanket woven of soft, dry sea grass. Later on, Demon finally set out to explore. It felt good to wiggle his bare toes in the soft, springy grass and feel the herb-scented breeze on his face. Being underwater was all very well for a while, but he definitely missed the smell of fresh air.

Unfortunately, just as he was walking back to see if the sleds of supplies had arrived, he had a nasty surprise. As the sun was setting in a blaze of red and pink clouds, a bright light began to shine on the path in front of him. Demon stopped and stared as the bright light took on the shape of a door, and a tall, dark-haired god with a crown of sun rays stepped out of it. It was Helios, Poseidon's deadly race rival. Demon stared, his mouth hanging open. How in Zeus's name had he done that? Surely even gods couldn't just make doors in the air wherever they wanted?

"Why, if it isn't young Pandemonius," Helios said, baring his white teeth in a friendly grin that somehow looked menacing. "Like my little trick, do you?"

Demon nodded. Well, it *was* pretty amazing.

The god lowered his head. "Not many people know my secret," he whispered. "But I'm sure you'll keep it to yourself. You see, I can make a door anywhere the sun's rays can touch. Useful, eh?"

Demon nodded again as Helios took his elbow in a firm grip so he couldn't escape.

"Now, you're just the boy I wanted. We have important things to discuss." Demon's stomach tried to leap sideways in fright. In his experience, discussing important things with a god almost

always led to the kind of trouble that left him worrying about being frazzled to a frizzle.

"The thing is," said the god, "I have a small problem. Here you are, looking after old Father Fishface's Hippocamps, but, as I understand it, you're the official stable boy to the gods, aren't you? Gods, meaning more than one god . . ."

"W-w-well, y-yes, Y-y-your Sh-sh-shining S-s-serenity." Demon gulped. "I-I s-suppose I am."

Helios smiled again. It was not a nice smile at all. Demon's knees began to tremble. "Oh, good," the god said. "I so hoped you'd say that. You won't mind popping down to the Stables of the Sun for an hour or so, then, and mending one of my celestial horses? Poor Abraxas has gone dreadfully lame, you see. Stepped on a sharp bit of star, or something. I'm sure that magical silver box of yours can fix him in two shakes of a comet's tail, though. Why don't you run along and fetch it, and then we'll be off? Quick as you can, now. I'll be waiting."

Poor Demon! He had no choice, but as he ran back toward where he'd left the Hippocamps, his mind was racing frantically. What if the box hadn't arrived? What if he couldn't cure Helios's horse without it? Even worse, what if Poseidon found out he was working for the other side?

"I'm doomed," he groaned as he ran into the stables, heart thumping like a maenad's drum. "Doomed."

"Why are you doomed?" asked a familiar high little voice. "What's happened now?"

"Oh, Eunice," he said miserably, slumping down onto one of the sleds, which, he was thankful to see, had now arrived. "I don't know what to do." Eunice came to perch beside him as he explained.

"Well," she said, tapping one small pearly tooth with a sharp fingernail, "I don't see what harm

it can do if you just go for an hour or two. Cure
Helios's horse and come straight back. Poseidon
need never know—he and Queen Amphitrite
are busy arranging all the stuff for the big party,
anyway. I'll start the unpacking and look after the
Hippocamps, don't worry." Just then, there was a
muffled squawk from behind them. Demon turned
around. There was the silver box, wriggling in its
seaweed bonds and flashing an angry red.

"Implementing emergency escape mode," it said
as several pairs of sharp scissors squeezed out from
under its lid and started snipping away at both the
kelp ropes and its waterproof cover.

Demon smiled gratefully at Eunice. "Thanks,"
he said. "You're a . . . a . . . real starfish. I'll be back
as soon as I can." Now that he had the box, he was
sure he really could cure Helios's horse—maybe
things would be okay after all.

"Hello, box," he said, helping it unravel itself

completely and lifting it into his arms as soon as the scissors had retracted. "Come on, we've got work to do." The silver box snarled a cross metallic snarl as Demon ran, bobbing and bumping over the short, springy grass toward the god of the sun. He sighed. The box was clearly in a temper again.

Demon stumbled at the god's heels as they went through Helios's midair door. He felt like he was being bathed in warm spring sunshine. On the other side was a gleaming stable block. Its roof was held up on towering ivory columns. The walls were scattered with glittering flakes of gold and were built of fire-colored marble. The door to each stall was marked with a big bronze flame. Beside the stable, a big flat pasture filled with waving grass and flocks of silvery sheep and goats stretched as far as the eye could see. A truly massive golden chariot was parked by one of the many open barns. Six huge horses had their heads down in the meadow nearby, grazing hungrily, as nymphs bathed the steeds' sweaty sides with water from crystal basins.

"Hey, 'Petia," called Helios. "Bring Abraxas over here, will you?" One of the nymphs set down her basin and led her charge toward Demon and the sun god. Demon could see the big stallion limping badly.

"Oh, dear," he said. "That must hurt."

"It does," whinnied Abraxas pitifully. "A lot."

"Put him in a stall," Helios commanded. "I just need to have another quick word with young Pandemonius here." Demon looked at him nervously. What did Helios want now? The god gripped him by the elbow again, and bent in close. "How are my friends the Cattle of the Sun doing?" the god asked unexpectedly. "Enjoying the nice bales of hay I send up from my fields, are they? Free of stomach gas? Keeping the goddesses happy at the lack of SMELL?"

"Y-y-yes, Your Sparkling Sunniness. Th-th-they're f-fine," Demon stammered, wondering what in Zeus's underpants the Cattle of the Sun had to do with anything. He soon found out.

"Glad to hear it," said Helios. "Now, here's the thing. I might find I have a bit of a problem getting that hay up to Olympus, say, if I heard that old Fish Father's Hippocamps were in tip-top condition for the race. On the other hand, if I heard that they'd had a recurrence of that nasty scale condition—been slowed down a bit by it, if you get my meaning—then I might find that the hay problem disappeared." His grip tightened, and he swung Demon around to face him, piercing him with a bright golden glare. "You understand me, young stable boy?" The god let him go and strode off around the corner of the stables. The nymphs followed. Demon thought he understood only too well. It didn't matter what he did now—whichever god won, he was either fated to be turned into a Demon-size smoking pile of charcoal by goddesses complaining about the terrible smell of gas coming from the Cattle of the Sun's bellies, or doomed to spend the next hundred years scrubbing salt off of seaweed.

CHAPTER 7

DEMON'S DREADFUL DILEMMA

Demon's feet dragged as he slowly approached the lame Abraxas. 'Petia the nymph had left with her sisters, and he was alone with the enormous stallion. "What am I going to do, box?" he asked quietly. The box whirred and flashed blue.

"Random inquiry matrix not enabled," said the box in its normal tinny tones. "Questions of a medical nature only accepted at the present time."

"Some help you are," Demon growled as he flipped the catch on the stall and went inside.

Bending down, he dumped the box on the golden straw and put his hand on Abraxas's lame leg. It was very hot, and the fetlock had swollen up. "Help me with a cure for this, then," he said crossly. The box clicked and whirred as blue symbols flashed on its lid, and then it shot open with a clang, making the stallion back up nervously, half rearing. Demon just barely managed to roll out of the way as a pair of enormous gold-shod hooves clattered past his face.

"Whoa! Whoa!" he said in his most soothing voice, grabbing at the halter. "Calm down, Abraxas. It's only my silly old box having a look at your sick foot. It didn't mean to scare you."

"Well, it did," whinnied a horsey voice high above Demon's head. "Nasty blue thing. I shall kick it, if it does it again." The box scuttled out of the way like a crab, hurriedly dumping a bowl, a pair of tweezers, a big bunch of green bandages, and a large packet of what looked like pink mud at Demon's feet.

"Analysis implemented. Foreign stellar object detected in equine subject. Initiate interactive solution immediately," it said in a snarky metallic gabble. Then it squeezed out of the stall and shut itself down in a sulk. Luckily, Demon had been with the box long enough to understand its strange language.

"You've got a bit of star stuck in your foot, I think," he said, picking up the huge hoof to inspect it underneath. Sure enough, there was something sparkling caught there. Working quickly, he pulled the dazzling fragment of star out gently with the tweezers. He then put a pink mud poultice on the sore part before winding some of the cooling green bandages around the hot fetlock. A large, soft muzzle snorted fragrant hay-scented air down the neck of his tunic.

"Thank you, Demon," Abraxas snuffled. "That feels much better. I must have stepped on a pointy bit of the Milky Way by mistake. Now I shall be able to race perfectly against Poseidon's Hippocamps."

Demon sighed. He'd forgotten about the race for a second.

As Demon led Abraxas slowly into his pasture, the other horses all crowded around.

"We've heard good things about you from our friends the winged horses!" they neighed. "They say you're the best stable boy they've ever had! Can't you come and live with us for a bit? It's boring having no one but the nymphs to talk to. No one ever comes to visit us here. All we ever get to do is pull the sun across the sky—and that's hard work!"

Demon smiled. "I'd love to," he said, "but the gods keep me very busy, you know, and I've got to get back to Poseidon's stables soon." His face fell

as he thought about his problem. "And now your master has asked me to do something awful to the Hippocamps."

"What? What?" they whinnied.

"If I make the Hippocamps ill again," Demon explained, "well . . . I'll . . . I'll be as bad as that horrible Heracles!"

The huge horses began to swish their tails angrily. "Helios can't make you do that," they neighed. "Making beasts sick is wrong."

"I KNOW!" Demon groaned. "But how do I get out of it?"

The horses went into a huddle, nickering softly to one another. Then Abraxas raised his head. "We'll help you stand up to our master, Demon," he whinnied. "But you'll have to be clever. You'll have to trick a god, and so will we."

"I can be clever," said Demon, crossing his fingers in hope that he could. As Abraxas quietly explained their plan, his whiskery muzzle tickled Demon's ear. Maybe this could work. By the time Helios came striding across the pasture, Demon knew exactly what he had to do. He walked forward to meet the sun god, with the six white horses making a solid, comforting line behind him.

"What's this?" said Helios. "You horses all look very serious for this time of night!" He frowned, bright sparks flashing from his eyebrows. "And so do you, young Pandemonius." Demon took a deep breath. Maybe it would be his last, if Helios didn't buy his story. But somehow he didn't care. He'd do what was right, even if he did end up as a pile of ash.

"Well, it's like this, Your Solar Godnificence," he said in a rush. "Your horses and I don't think I should do what you asked. M-my job is making beasts well, not ill. Poseidon would suspect you immediately. B-b-but I think m-maybe I can help you win in another way." He stepped backward into the line of horses and crossed his fingers tightly.

But Helios was looking at his horses.

"Well, my celestial steeds!" he snarled. "And what will you do if I say no to this son of Pan?"

"Then the sun's chariot will not run across the sky till you agree," neighed all six horses together.

"So! Even YOU betray me!" shouted the sun god angrily.

There was a sudden blast of heat, and Demon smelled burning as the edges of his tunic begin to singe and smolder. He began to talk very fast.

"There's a magic herb," he gabbled, batting at the sparks frantically. "It makes beasts run faster than the North Wind if you paint the juice of it on their hooves. I-I can get it for you."

Helios grabbed him and lifted him up by the front of his tunic, leaving his bare legs kicking and dangling. "What is this herb?" he growled. "I've never heard of such a thing."

"I-i-it's c-called G-gorgos Anemos, and it c-comes from the kingdom of the Old Man of the Sea."

Helios threw him down in the grass. "Very well," he growled. "But mark me well, stable boy. If my horses don't run faster than light itself in that race, I will personally see to it that you are set as a spot in the heart of the sun to burn for all eternity!" With that, Helios opened another door in the air and shoved Demon through to Poseidon's island. The silver box came tumbling after him.

Demon gulped and gasped, scrambling and stumbling back down the narrow, rocky path to the stables. The first part of the plan had worked. Now he just had to persuade Eunice to help him with the second, but it would have to wait till the morning. He was too tired to do anything but lie down on his pallet and go to sleep.

A strong smell of seaweed met him as he woke up the next morning. Yawning, he rolled out of bed and jumped down into the stables. The Hippocamps all had their noses buried in their mangers, and Eunice was perched on a rock, playing a little flute crusted with shells.

"Goodness," she gasped, dropping the flute with a crunch. "Whatever happened to your tunic?"

Demon glanced down. There *were* a few big burn holes in it, and some finger-shaped scorch marks. "Helios got a bit angry with me," he said. "I've sort of played a trick on him, and I need you to help me with the next part of it."

Eunice turned pale green. "Me?" she asked nervously. "Why me? What can *I* do?"

"Well," he said, taking a deep breath and hoping.

"Do you by any chance know where the Old Man of the Sea lives?"

Then Eunice did the last thing he expected. She laughed. "Well, of course I do, silly," she said. "He's my dad."

Demon goggled at her. "But . . . but . . . I thought your father was called Nereus!"

"He is. But because he's so ancient and wise, lots of people call him the Old Man of the Sea, too. What do you need him for?"

"Helios's horses told me that a magic herb called Gorgos Anemos grows in his kingdom, and I need it for my trick to work."

Eunice's mouth fell open in shock. "Gorgos Anemos?" Eunice shrieked. "B-but that's our swiftweed flower. No one's supposed to know about that but my family. NO ONE! How did those wretched celestial horses find out about it, by Hades's toenails?" She dived off the rock and swam over to him. "I think you'd better tell me all about this trick you've come up with at ONCE," she said. So Demon explained.

"The horses want it to be a fair race with no cheating," he said. "So although I'm going to paint their hooves with the magic liquid and they'll do what Helios wants and gallop faster than ever before, I'm also going to put it on the Hippocamps' hooves and flippers—only Helios won't know that. So I won't have to make the Hippocamps ill again, and whichever god wins will truly have the honestly fastest team."

"It's still very dangerous," said Eunice. "What if Helios finds out about the family secret? Even worse, if he loses, he's bound to be furious, anyway, and turn you into a sunspot."

Demon thought it was best not to mention at this point that he'd already told Helios about the magic herb—well, how was *he* to have known it was a secret?

"The thing is," he said instead, "Zeus will be at the race, and everyone knows he hates cheating. If Helios loses and comes after me, the horses have promised to threaten him with Zeus's wrath. I-I just have to take the risk. It's only a stupid race, and I won't hurt a beast deliberately, not for any god!"

Eunice sighed. "All right, then. Let's hitch up the Hippocamps and find my dad," she said. "Though if he ever finds out that I'm using the swiftweed for anyone other than family, I'll probably be shut in a cave for a million years and have to marry the giant squid."

CHAPTER 8
THE OLD MAN OF THE SEA

Demon and Eunice harnessed all nine Hippocamps to the chariot. It was the perfect excuse to exercise them, just as Poseidon had instructed.

They squashed in, with Demon at the reins, then shot out of the stables and into the open air, splishing and sploshing over the crests of the waves. It was very strange being in the driver's seat, but Demon soon got used to it, though he didn't dare go as fast as Poseidon.

"Which way?" he yelled, spitting out a mouthful

of seawater.

"Straight on!" Eunice yelled over his shoulder, her dark-green hair flying in the breeze. Soon Demon began to enjoy himself, and as he got more confident, they went faster and faster, zipping past islands and racing dolphins and sea-skimming seagulls. Then, just as they reached two huge red spires of rock sticking up out of the ocean, Eunice shouted, "Dive!"

They shot downward, then leveled out and

began cantering along a white, sandy road at the
bottom of the sea. Demon held the mass of reins
tightly and kept the Hippocamps going straight.
Looking out of the corners of his eyes, he saw a tall
green forest of kelp trees, their trunks wavering in
the current, and colorful rippling anemones set in
clumps at their roots. Small sea horses, like living
jewels, flitted through the branches. They came

to perch on Demon's head and shoulders, making tiny shrill squeaks of joy. Then the forest thinned, turning into a series of large meadows of sea grass where herds of strange-looking sea monsters with hairy nostrils, crayfish tails, and rows of neat webbed feet were grazing. Then Demon saw a large cave ahead.

"That's my dad's house," said Eunice.

"What should I say?" he asked.

"Leave it to me," said Eunice. "My dad can be a bit funny sometimes. The only thing you have to remember is never to accept his challenge to a wrestling contest. He always wins—and he always cheats!" Demon would have liked to hear more, but Eunice was already slipping out of the chariot and tying the Hippocamps up to a barnacle-encrusted ring.

"Stay there!" Demon said to them sternly as he scrambled out after her. The Hippocamps looked at him sideways, put their heads down, and started tearing up sea grass.

"Hey, Dad! Where are you? It's me, Eunice! I've brought a friend to visit," she called, swimming into the cave. Demon followed clumsily after her. The cave was dimly lit by angler fish set in niches in the walls. It had a far more homey feel than Poseidon's palace. There were bits of wrecked ships serving as chairs and tables, and some rather rickety shell ornaments—clearly made by Eunice and her sisters—dotted the floor and the driftwood shelves.

"In here," came a booming voice.

"This way," Eunice hissed, beckoning Demon into a smaller cave. Stooped over a pile of black horned objects was the Old Man of the Sea. His long hair was tied back with a string of bladder wrack, and his beard was knotted with shells and small starfish. In his hand he had a large needle threaded with an array of sparkling jewels. Eunice grinned.

"Decorating purses for the mermaids again, Dad?" she asked. Nereus grunted.

"Careless girls are always losing 'em," he said. "I never have enough in stock." He looked up at Demon. "Who's this, then? Some young whippersnapper come to challenge me, I suppose."

"No! Of course not, Dad. This is Demon, Pan's son. He's looking after Poseidon's Hippocamps for now, but he's really the stable boy to Olympus. He's a great healer, too."

Nereus looked at Demon from under bushy eyebrows. "You sure you don't want to wrestle me, son?"

Demon shook his head, remembering what Eunice had told him. "Not really, thank you very much, Your Ancientness. I'm a bit short for it."

"Well, you're no Heracles, that's for sure. Wretched heroes—I hate 'em. Always wanting something for nothing. Suppose you want something, too, do you?" Demon was about to answer when Eunice trod hard on his toe with one of her flipper feet.

"No, no," she said airily. "Demon just wanted to see where I used to live. We were exercising the Hippocamps and thought we'd drop by for a visit. But now that you mention it, I could do with a bit of swiftweed juice for my dolphin. Poor old Seapetal's fins are getting a bit creaky. We can't keep up with my sisters anymore, so I want to rub some on him before we go for our next ride." She beamed up at her father lovingly. "I know you don't give it out to just anybody, but surely I can have some. I am your

- 379 -

favorite daughter, after all!" Nereus stared at her suspiciously.

"Swiftweed juice, eh? Dangerous stuff, that. You be careful with it. Use a seagull-feather brush to put it on like I taught you, and don't use too much, or the poor beast will take off like a rocket." He glared ferociously at Demon. "And don't you go telling anyone about it, either, young Demon. It's meant to be a family secret, that juice is, and Eunice here had no business talking about it in front of you. If that wretched Heracles or any of the other heroes get to hear about it, I'll have them tromping down here in droves, wanting some to make their stupid arrows fly faster, or something."

"Don't worry, I'd never tell anyone. I don't like Heracles, either," said Demon. "He's always bashing up my beasts."

"Well, see that you don't. Or I'll turn you into a clam." The Old Man of the Sea moved across to a large alcove set in the rock and picked up a crystal jug full of bright orange liquid.

"Here," said Eunice, pulling out a large bottle with a carved stone stopper from inside her robe. "You can put it in this." She reached up and gave him a kiss on his hairy cheek. "Thanks, you're the best dad in the world."

"You and your little tricks." He chuckled, handing her the filled bottle. "Now get away with you, child, and give my love to your sisters. Tell them to come visit soon. Amphitrite keeps all of you too busy!"

"I will," said Eunice, pulling Demon out of the cave and toward the tethered Hippocamps. "I promise." She put her finger to her lips as soon as they were around the corner and out of sight. "Don't say anything. The walls have ears," she whispered, nodding toward the angler fish lights.

Eunice slipped out of the chariot as soon as

they drove into the palace stables. "I'd better go and check on Amphitrite. She said I still had to do my duties for her, even if I was helping you. I'll be down again as quick as I can—sorry to leave you with all the work." Fumbling in the pocket of her robe, she thrust the bottle of swiftweed juice at him. "Hide this in a safe place, and DON'T use it till I can show you how." Then she shot off before he could say a single word. Demon shoved the bottle under a bale of silver seaweed as the Hippocamps began to prance and dance with impatience to get to their mangers. He'd deal with it later.

Demon felt a bit lonely once he'd finished seeing to the Hippocamps. They weren't very good company—they only spoke in single words, and he missed the griffin's snarky chat. He got out the bottle of swiftweed juice and looked over at the box, which was still on the high rocky shelf where he'd left it. "Box," he said politely. "Would you mind keeping this safe for me? It's pretty dangerous stuff, apparently, and I need to make sure that nobody but Eunice or me uses it."

The silver box shuddered and let out a couple of blue sparks, but eventually its lid opened with a cross-sounding creak. "Insert object," it said, rather grudgingly. Demon placed the bottle inside, and immediately the lid snapped shut. The box began to hum busily. "Poison protocols in process," it announced, just as a flashing red skull and crossbones appeared on each of its sides. Demon patted it, then yelped as a strange tingly shock passed through his hand.

"Ouch!" he yelled.

"Safety procedures present and correct." The box glowed. "Item now password protected."

"Password?" asked Demon angrily, sucking his sore fingers. "What's the password?"

"Mother's name plus father's gift," it whirred.

Demon thought for a moment, puzzled. Then it suddenly came to him. "Er, that would be . . . er . . . Carys and Pan pipes," he said.

"Correct. Do you wish to retrieve item?"

"No, not now. You keep it safe. Thanks, box. You're the best." The box glowed bright blue with pleasure.

CHAPTER 9

THE SWIFTWEED TEST

The stables were spick and span; the Hippocamps were happy, polished, exercised, and fed. Demon wondered what to do next. He wasn't used to having only one set of beasts to look after. Should he try to find Eunice? Should he report to Poseidon? Or should he find the kitchens? Since he was now hungrier than a pack of ravening manticores, and his stomach was in danger of sticking to his spine, he decided that finding the kitchens was pretty urgent.

"I don't suppose you know where the kitchens are," he asked the Hippocamps.

"KITCHENS! FOOD! YUM!" they squealed. Demon rolled his eyes.

"You're hopeless," he sighed. "I guess I'll have to find them myself." But just then, Eunice came into the stables with five of her sisters. They were all riding dolphins, and Eunice had another one on a silver rein.

"Come on, Demon," she called. "I've brought Seawhistle for you to ride. Amphitrite wants us to collect some shells for decorating the banqueting hall. There's a perfect beach on the island next door." Unfortunately, Demon's stomach gave an enormous gurgle right as she stopped talking, and the Nereids all giggled.

"I think he's hungry again," said the one in the pink robe.

"Poor boy," said the one in yellow. "Haven't you

been feeding him, Eunice?" Demon felt his face getting redder than the setting sun as he climbed onto Seawhistle's back.

"I can perfectly well feed myself!" he snapped, wriggling himself into place behind the big back fin. "It's just that I haven't quite found out where the kitchens are yet."

Eunice laughed. "Well, that's easy enough," she said. "Let's go there before we start on the shells."

The palace kitchens were amazing. Pots and pans full of delicious-looking things bounced and boiled on top of jets of scalding water, and piles of strange-looking sea vegetables were being chopped and shaped and stuffed, along with endless baskets of shellfish. There was even a huge cotton candy castle being decorated with edible shells and strands of seaweed. Poseidon's cooks seemed to be preparing enough food to feed a thousand gods and goddesses, and Demon's stomach was soon as full as it could be. Afterward, he found himself collecting shells on a little white sandy beach. The Nereids thought it was funny to pelt him with wet seaweed, but he soon repaid them by stuffing sand down the backs of their robes.

After that, Demon quickly fell into a routine. What with exercising the Hippocamps in the morning, getting them ready for Poseidon's daily inspection, then taking time off in the afternoons to ride Seawhistle and explore with Eunice and the other Nereids, the days before the race quickly passed. Despite what Eunice said about her sisters, they were fun to be with, always laughing and playing jokes as they showed him around the palace, challenged him to swimming races (which he always lost), and generally treated him like a long-lost younger brother. But the night before the race, he started to get a nasty sinking feeling of doom in his stomach.

As he was giving the Hippocamps their last feed, he was surprised to see Eunice ride in on her dolphin, Seapetal, with Seawhistle swimming behind her. By that time he had rumpled his hair into a tangled bird's nest.

"What are you doing here?" he asked, as nasty, wriggly worry things joined the feeling of doom. "Is-is-is something wrong?"

"No, nothing's *wrong*, except that my sisters are all fluffing and faffing and looking at stupid jewels," she said. "Luckily, Amphitrite is too busy choosing which dress to wear tomorrow to notice I'm not there, so I thought I'd escape. Want to take Seawhistle for a night ride? There's a lovely full moon, and the stars are much brighter than Halia's silly old opals." Then she frowned, looking at him. "What's the matter, Demon? Why is your hair all sticky-uppy like that?"

"What if the swiftweed juice doesn't work?" he burst out. "What if it's a bad batch or something? What if Poseidon and Helios find out? What if the effect runs out halfway through the race . . . ?" Eunice rode over and grabbed his shoulder, giving him a little shake.

"You big silly," she said. "Of course it'll work—it lasts for a whole day, usually. And I'll be there to help with the Hippocamps. You'll see—it'll all be fine. But if you're really worried, we can try out a tiny drop on Seapetal and Seawhistle here. They won't tell anyone, will you, boys?" The dolphins opened their mouths and grinned, shaking their heads violently.

"Race you," they whistled to each other. "Last one back's a barnacle's bottom!"

Eunice was very impressed with the box's security measures. "It's better than a whole legion of those stupid Triton guards," she said as the bottle of swiftweed appeared, making the box glow with pleasure again. Taking a tiny seagull-feather brush from her pocket, she dipped just the very tip into the bottle and painted a minuscule amount onto the dolphins' front flippers and tails before putting everything back.

"Now," she said, jumping onto her dolphin's back, "let's race." Demon hardly had time to scramble onto Seawhistle before Eunice and Seapetal shot out of the stables faster than Zeus's lightning bolts. Seawhistle followed, streaking past his friend as Demon clung on for dear life. Right out into the ocean they raced, following the silvery path of the full moon. The stars zipped past in a blur overhead as the dolphins whistled and clicked with glee, overtaking shoals of very surprised-looking fish, and jumping high in the air. By the time they turned back, Demon had no more worries about whether the swiftweed would work or not. It was fantastic stuff! But as they came into view of the palace, they saw an extraordinary sight. A column of rainbow-colored light streamed down from the moonlit heavens and into the palace, lighting up the sky. Demon reined Seawhistle to a halt, Eunice slowing beside him.

"Whatever is THAT?" asked Eunice, shading her eyes.

"Gods!" Seawhistle whistled, dancing among the waves.

"Goddesses!" clicked Seapetal. "Lots of them."

Demon recognized the multicolored light. "It's the Iris Express from Olympus. I'd better start getting the Hippocamps ready. Poseidon will be coming to get the chariot soon." He gulped. "I-I just hope Helios doesn't arrive at the same time."

"Oh no!" gasped Eunice. "I've got to get back to the queen. If the gods and goddesses are arriving already, Amphitrite will definitely notice that I'm not there. She's bound to be fussing that Aphrodite has a better dress for the feast, or something stupid. Come on, Seapetal, quick! I'll see you later, Demon—and DON'T WORRY!" Her voice faded into the distance as Demon headed more slowly to the stables.

Even though Demon knew now that the swiftweed worked, he was still nervous. To keep himself occupied, he polished the sleepy Hippocamps over and over till their bronze scales shone. Even the fiercest one was used to him now, and it nuzzled his pockets for the purple seaberry treats he'd taken to bringing them from the kitchen. Just as he was going to get the harnesses ready, there was a blaze of light in the cave entrance.

"Time to keep your promise, stable boy," Helios said as he appeared through his door in the air, smiling his dangerously white smile. "I do hope you succeeded in getting what you needed from the Old Man of the Sea. It would be such a shame to turn you into a sunspot when it seems you've worked so hard polishing up those stupid sea steeds for his Foolish Fishiness." He smirked. "It won't help them go faster, though, will it?"

"N-no, Your Sunshiny Superbness. It definitely

won't." It wasn't a lie, Demon thought. Shininess *wouldn't* help the Hippocamps go faster. "I-I'll just go g-g-get the magic juice." Taking a deep breath to calm himself, he whispered the password to the box, got the swiftweed juice out, and put it safely inside his robe, together with the seagull-feather paintbrush. "Ready," he said, scrambling up onto the rock, hoping that Poseidon wouldn't come to the stables and find him gone. Helios grabbed his hand and pulled him through the door to the other side. Waiting just outside were the six golden-maned celestial horses, each with a nymph at its head. They were already harnessed to the gigantic Chariot of the Sun, which had a long braided rope snaking out behind it into the distance. Demon could see the top of a shining golden ball just poking over the horizon.

"Hurry up, boy," snapped Helios. "Dawn waits for no god, and she'll be going to the starting line

soon." He seemed nervous, but not as nervous as Demon, whose hands were shaking as he brushed each shining golden hoof with a drop of swiftweed juice. Abraxas bent his head and brushed Demon comfortingly with his white muzzle, but he didn't say anything. It was too dangerous with Helios so near. Finally Demon finished and stood up. The horses were now pawing restlessly at the ground, their skins rippling and shuddering.

"All done, Your Celestial Cloudlessness," he said, stuffing the bottle and brush back into his tunic. Helios stepped forward, leaning over him until they were nearly nose to nose. Demon could feel the heat of the sun god's gaze singeing his eyebrows, but he didn't dare move.

"And can you swear to me that they'll run faster than they ever have before, stable boy?" he asked softly, his voice as menacing as the giant scorpion's sting.

"Y-y-yes," Demon stammered. "Faster than the North and South Winds together, I swear. You'll notice the difference in them immediately." He just hoped the Hippocamps would run equally as fast.

"They'd better, or you'll be a crispy sunspot by sundown!" With one last threatening glare, Helios pushed Demon back through the door.

"I wish his own sun would burn him to a crisp," Demon muttered angrily. "I'm fed up with gods pushing me around and bullying me." He went to get the harnesses in a very grumpy mood.

CHAPTER 10

THE RACE OF SEA AND SUN

As Demon finished polishing the very last buckle, Poseidon whirled into the cave, golden trident in hand, his beard bristling and crackling with energy.

"Good, good," he said. "Glad to see you've got everything in tip-top condition early, Pandemonius. We don't want to be outshone by those celestial beasties, do we?"

Demon shook his head. "Definitely not, Your Marine Magnificence," he said.

"You can bring the chariot around to the east side of the island now. Eos is going to start the race just as dawn breaks. We're going to show that stupid Sun Boy show-off who's fastest, aren't we, my lovelies?" said the sea god as he visited each Hippocamp's stall.

"GO FAST! FAST! FAST! FAST!" they trumpeted, beginning to rear and plunge.

"Calm down, calm down! Save your energy for the race!" Poseidon boomed, patting Demon on the shoulder. "I'll see you there, stable boy. Now I've got to go and greet my fellow gods." He frowned. "Not my kind of thing, but Amphitrite insists we do things properly. Says Olympus will look down on us if we don't." With that, he disappeared in a sparkling whoosh of seawater.

Should he put the swiftweed juice on the Hippocamps now? Demon wondered. No. That wouldn't do at all. Helios was bound to think it was suspicious if they galloped up to the starting line too fast. He'd have to sneak it on at the last minute without Helios seeing. His heart began to thunder like a whole herd of centaurs. However was he going to pull this off?

With trembling fingers, he harnessed the excited Hippocamps to the chariot, then got in and headed for the east side of the island. Driving up onto a shallow beach in the gray light before the dawn, he jumped out and stood ready by the Hippocamps' heads. Up on the cliff above was a huge crowd of gods and goddesses seated on a bank of seats covered in silken cushions. Craning his neck, he spotted Zeus's crown of lightning bolts—and was that Hera beside him, waving a fan of peacock feathers and talking to Poseidon and Amphitrite? He scuttled around to the other side of the Hippocamps. He didn't want *her* spotting him! Then he noticed something else. Making her way down the cliff path was a tall goddess dressed in palest pink. Eos, goddess of dawn, was on her way to start the race. He looked around him frantically. Where was Eunice? He couldn't do this without her help, and time was running out!

Luckily, just then, a breathless Eunice swam up on Seapetal. "Have you put it on them?" she hissed at him as she slid off the dolphin's back.

"No," said Demon. "Helios's horses are done, but I haven't had a chance to do the Hippocamps yet. I was waiting for you. Quick! Hold on to them while I pretend to inspect their hooves and tails." Working fast, and keeping a nervous eye out for Helios and his chariot, Demon daubed a drop of swiftweed juice onto each tail, fin, and hoof. Just as he'd finished the last Hippocamp, he saw Poseidon striding toward him across the sand. He shoved the bottle and brush back into his tunic as the Hippocamps beside him started to act even more like high-strung thoroughbreds than usual. Their front hooves were pawing at the sand, and their tails thrashed the water behind, making the chariot toss and sway in the waves. The swiftweed was definitely taking effect! Demon held the chariot steady as Poseidon climbed in.

"Whoa!" he yelled as the Hippocamps plunged and reared with impatience to be off. "Whoa, you eager beasties!" He waved frantically to Eos as a tiny rim of light appeared on the horizon, six white horses silhouetted against its brightness. Helios had arrived! "Ready when you are, Sun Boy," Poseidon shouted, voice booming across the waves as he raised his trident. "I can hardly hold mine back— you don't have a chance with those celestial nags of yours!"

The sun god laughed rudely. "Eat my spray, Fish Father!" he yelled back, cracking his starry whip so that his horses reared in their traces.

"On your marks," shouted Eos, raising her arms in the air. "Get set! GO!" Out of her fingers shot beams of pink radiance, which lit up the whole sky.

The Hippocamps hurtled forward in a froth of foam, just as Helios's team streaked away in the distance. Within seconds they were out of sight over the western horizon, roared on by a crowd of gods standing on the hill above the shore and a cheering mass of sea folk bobbing in the waves. The race was on!

"Let's go and find my sisters," said Eunice. "You can't do anything more now, and we might be able to see more from up there." Together, they climbed the little path up the cliff, Eunice stumbling a bit on her flipper feet. Demon grabbed her arm as she nearly tripped on a rock.

"Oops!" she said, wincing. "I'm not really used to walking on this stony stuff. It feels like knives digging into me." Demon hadn't really thought about that.

"Do you want a piggyback ride?" he asked.

"Yes, please!" she said gratefully. So Demon,

wheezing and panting a bit, carried her up the cliff. She was a lot more solid than she looked, and he was quite glad to set her down on the soft grass at the top. Squeezing past a mass of nymphs and fauns who were chattering and shoving each other and standing on tiptoe to see something just in front of them, Eunice and Demon ended up by the crowd of seated gods and goddesses. Zeus was standing on a disk of air in front of them, his hands creating what looked like a picture in the air—a huge revolving blue globe, with white at the top and bottom, and lots of large, green, strangely shaped blobs set in the blue bits. Two fiery dots—one gold, one silver—were moving across it, leaving a trail behind them. The gold dot was slightly in front of the silver one, and the two trails led back to one flashing red beacon. All the gods and goddesses were yelling for their favorites.

"Come on, Poseidon," shouted a deep voice

just above Demon's head. He looked up and saw a familiar figure with a black beard and a dirty face. It was his friend Hephaestus! He reached up and tugged on the smith god's robe.

"Hello, Heffy," he called. Hephaestus looked down, frowning, but when he saw Demon, his soot-stained face broke into a broad grin.

"Well, if it isn't young Pandemonius," he said. "What are you doing down there, you cheeky brat? And who's your friend?"

Demon introduced Eunice, who smiled nervously.

"Ah, one of the Nereids, are you?" said the smith god, nodding his head wisely. Then he turned back to Demon, a stern look on his face. "There's been an awful lot of noise coming from the Stables lately, young man—you should keep those beasts of yours under better control."

"I haven't been there," he said, hastily explaining

about Poseidon and the Hippocamps. "Hermes was supposed to send someone called Autolykos to look after the beasts." He looked worried. "Maybe he hasn't been looking after them properly. Er, there hasn't been a smell of . . . you know . . . has there?"

"What, poo? Not that I've noticed," said Hephaestus. He looked over at Zeus's picture. "Come ON, Poseidon," he roared, shaking his fist in the air.

"Er, excuse me, Your Godnificence," said Eunice timidly. "What is that round thing?"

"That? Why, that's a picture of the whole world, of course, sea child." He pointed to the two moving dots. "There's Poseidon, see? He's the silver dot. And there's Helios. He's the gold dot. Where we are now is the red dot—and that's the start and finish line. Zeus is judging the race, you know—and this way we can all see there's no cheating." He cleared his throat and looked around, lowering his voice slightly. "I've wagered Ares one of my magic suits of armor that Poseidon will win. He's supporting Helios, of course, but I reckon Poseidon has the edge. Helios's horses are ahead now, but they've got that heavy sun to pull, remember, and I think they'll be all out of steam by dusk." Demon said nothing, but he heaved a deep sigh. He was pretty much in trouble, whichever god lost.

The lead changed several times throughout that long day. Finally, the silver and gold trails were almost at the red dot again, and as the sun sank toward the west, the gods and goddesses cheered even louder, shaking the earth with their cries. Demon's heart began to pound in his chest. Helios's gold dot was just in front, but Poseidon's silver one was creeping up on it. Then, with a flash of light, the two teams burst over the eastern horizon. Zeus raised his hand, and a bolt of lightning sizzled and hissed as it hit the waves, laying out a long red finish line in front of the two teams of galloping steeds. Poseidon's trident streamed with blue fire, which whipped out over the Hippocamps' heads, as Helios urged his horses on with a crack of starlight. Slowly, inch by inch, the Hippocamps were catching the celestial horses, and Demon found his fists were clenched so hard that his fingernails dug painfully into his palms.

"Come on, come on, come ON," he muttered as Eunice shrieked and danced beside him. With a last, mighty effort, the Hippocamps drew level with their rivals, and as their noses touched the lightning finish line, two identical spears of red flame shot into the air beside each chariot.

Zeus's voice boomed like thunder as Helios and Poseidon reined their steeds to a halt. "I declare this race a DEAD HEAT!" he roared into a sudden silence. "You have BOTH won!"

Poseidon and Helios began to laugh at the

same time. "Good race, Sun Boy!" said the sea god, reaching over and holding out his hand to his rival deity.

"Good race, Fish Father," said Helios, leaning over and shaking it firmly. "The four Winds themselves couldn't have beaten either of us today. My horses have NEVER run so fast." His eyes sought out Demon in the crowd, and as the sun god gave him a nod, Demon felt a big burden of fear slip from his shoulders. He wouldn't be a sunspot or have to scrub seaweed after all!

CHAPTER 11

THE ORDER OF OCEAN

"Let us care for our gallant beasts," said Poseidon, raising his trident, "and then we will feast and salute each other's victory." Demon knew that was his signal. Heading down the cliff path again, he ran to the Hippocamps' heads. Their sides were heaving, and they looked tired, but Demon could see they were happy.

"HOORAY! HOORAY! HOORAY!" they whinnied as Helios and his horses finally pulled the sun beneath the horizon and dusk fell.

Poseidon clapped Demon on the shoulder. "Well done, stable boy," he said. "We didn't win, but we didn't lose, either. I've never known them to go so quick as they did today. Whatever you've been doing to them, it certainly paid off. Don't suppose I can persuade you to stay here and look after them full-time, can I?"

"Well, Your Mighty Marineness, I'd love to, really," said Demon carefully, "but I don't think Zeus would be very happy about it, and it wouldn't be fair to my beasts up on Olympus."

"Well, I suppose not. But if they get sick again, I'll be calling on you. You can be sure of that. Now take these poor beasties back to their stalls and give them a good feed and a rubdown. Then come back to the feast. You deserve a reward for all your hard work."

"SEAWEED! SPONGE! SLEEP!" neighed the Hippocamps eagerly as they galloped around the island to their stable. Demon took care of them, then made his way up to the banqueting hall, wiping the worst smears off his tunic as he went.

It was as magnificent as the undersea throne room. The towering walls were banded with stripes of lapis lazuli and mother-of-pearl, and under the pale-blue crystal ceiling, sparkling yellow stars whirled and shone, speckling the room with twinkles of moving light. Water lapped around tall columns of white coral, and on a raised dais carved with sea creatures was an enormous shell-decorated silver table where the gods and goddesses were sitting. Smaller silver tables led down in a series of steps from each end of the big table, eventually dipping down into the water so that the sea folk could eat comfortably.

Demon looked around the noisy room buzzing with chatter. Where should he sit? Then he spotted Eunice and her Nereid sisters, who were waving and beckoning from a table just below the dais. "Over here, Demon," they called.

Helios had decided that as he was joint victor, he'd bring half the feast from his kitchens. There was stuff Demon had never eaten before, but it all looked yummy. He wasted no time in filling his plate.

The evening passed in a blur of eating and drinking, and just as Demon was stuffing in one last morsel of sun cake, Poseidon banged on the floor with his trident. The whole banqueting hall shook.

"Brother Zeus," he said loudly. "I have borrowed your stable boy, and much as I should like to keep him, I must return him to Olympus. But first, I would like to reward him. Stand forth, Pandemonius, son of Pan."

Demon nearly choked. "What, me?" he whispered to Eunice. She gave him a little push.

"Yes, you! Go on, don't keep him waiting!"

Demon wriggled under the table and walked

up the steps, sandals sloshing slightly and very aware of his slightly grubby tunic, to kneel in front of Poseidon's seat. He didn't dare look up, with so many gods and goddesses staring at him.

"You have done me great service, son of Pan, and I hereby award you the Order of Ocean, and the freedom of my seas. You may also ask a reward of me." Demon did look up at that, totally amazed.

Poseidon was holding out a large speckled cowrie shell with golden edges, hanging from a heavy golden chain. Demon scrambled off his knees and leaned forward so the sea god could hang it around his neck.

"Now, Pandemonius, what reward can I give you? Jewels, pearls—perhaps some golden treasure?" Demon shook his head, speechless. He didn't need any of those things. Then he caught a glimpse of Eunice, and suddenly he knew exactly what he was going to ask for.

"Well, Your Serene Saltiness, maybe there's one thing. C-could you possibly make my friend Eunice the official Keeper of the Hippocamps? The Tritons don't seem that interested in looking after them, a-and Eunice is really very good with them and the d-dolphins—m-much better than she is at brushing hair." He stopped abruptly, aware that he was babbling a bit.

Poseidon laughed. "Very well," he said. "Come here, young Eunice. I can't say I'm very surprised after all the times my Amphitrite has complained about you running away to hang around my stables!" Eunice came up to the dais, beaming like the midday sun, and stopped by Demon's side.

"From this moment forward, Eunice the Nereid is official Handmaid to the Hippocamps and Damsel of the Dolphins," Poseidon announced, and the room erupted in loud claps and cheers as Demon and Eunice made their way back to their table, where Eunice's sisters were clapping loudest of all.

"Thanks," she whispered to Demon. "A proper job at last! I'm so happy, I could pop like a squashed sea slug!"

"Ugh! Gross!" he whispered back. But he didn't really mean it. He was too happy himself. Tomorrow he'd go back to the Stables on Olympus and sort out whatever mess Autolykos had made of them, but tonight . . . tonight he was going to celebrate his lucky escape from sunspots and seaweed-scrubbing with Eunice and all his new Nereid friends.

GLOSSARY

PRONUNCIATION GUIDE

THE GODS

Aphrodite (AF-ruh-DY-tee): Goddess of love and beauty and all things pink and fluffy.

Apollo (uh-POL-oh): The radiant god of music. More than a little sensitive to criticism.

Ares (AIR-eez): God of war. Loves any excuse to pick a fight.

Artemis (AR-te-miss): Goddess of the hunt. Can't decide if she wants to protect animals or kill them.

Athena (a-THEE-na): Goddess of wisdom and defender of pesky, troublesome heroes.

Chiron (KY-ron): God of the centaurs. Known for his wisdom and healing abilities.

Dionysus (DY-uh-NY-suss): God of wine. Turns even sensible gods into silly goons.

Eos (EE-oss): The Titan goddess of the dawn. Makes things rosy with a simple touch of her fingers.

Hades (HAY-deez): Zeus's brother and the gloomy, fearsome ruler of the Underworld.

Helios (HEE-lee-us): The bright, shiny, and blinding Titan god of the sun.

Hephaestus (hih-FESS-tuss): God of blacksmithing, metalworking, fire, volcanoes, and most things awesome.

Hera (HEER-a): Zeus's scary wife. Drives a chariot pulled by screechy peacocks.

Hermes (HUR-meez): The clever, fun-loving, jack-of-all-trades messenger god.

Hestia (HESS-tee-ah): Goddess of the hearth and home. Bakes the most heavenly treats.

Pan (PAN): God of shepherds and flocks. Frequently found wandering grassy hillsides, playing his pipes.

Persephone (per-SEFF-uh-NEE): Part-time goddess of the Underworld, part-time goddess of spring.

Poseidon (puh-SY-dun): God of the sea and controller of natural and supernatural events.

Zeus (ZOOSS): King of the gods. Fond of smiting people with lightning bolts.

OTHER MYTHICAL BEINGS

Amphitrite (am-fih-TRI-tee): Poseidon's wife and queen of the sea. A pretty high-maintenance lady.

Arachne (uh-RACK-nee): Used to be a weaving woman until she ticked off the gods. Now she's a weaving spider instead.

Autolykos (ow-TOL-ih-kohs): A trickster who shape-shifts his stolen goods to avoid getting caught.

Charon (CARE-un): The ferryman who rows the dead across the River Styx. One-way trips only.

Cherubs (CHAIR-ubs): Small flying babies. Mostly cute.

Delphinus (dell-FY-nuss): A messenger dolphin who helped play matchmaker between Poseidon and Amphitrite.

Dryads (DRY-ads): Tree nymphs. Can literally sing trees to life.

Epimetheus (ep-ee-MEE-thee-us): Prometheus's silly brother who designed animals. Thank him for giving us the platypus and naked mole rat.

Eurydice (yuh-RID-ih-see): Orpheus's true love. Enjoyed frolicking in the fields until she died of a snakebite.

Geryon (JAYR-ee-un): A cattle-loving giant with a two-headed dog.

Heracles (HAIR-a-kleez): The half-god "hero" who just *loooves* killing magical beasts.

Ixion (ick-SYE-on): King who pushed his father-in-law into a pit of hot coals. Now tied to a wheel in Tartarus for eternity.

Lethe (LEE-thee): Spirit of . . . something . . . can't remember . . . ah yes! The spirit of forgetfulness.

Midas (MY-dus): A king who foolishly wished for everything he touched to turn to gold.

Naiads (NYE-adz): Fresh-water nymphs: keeping Olympus clean and refreshed since 500 BC.

Nereids (NEER-ee-idz): A sisterhood of fifty sea nymphs who love to gossip.

Nereus (NEER-ee-uss): The Old Man of the Sea. Though, with fifty daughters, they ought to call him the Old Dad of the Sea.

Nymphs (NIMFS): Giggly, girly, dancing nature spirits.

Orion (uh-RY-un): A giant heroic huntsman, best known for wearing a belt made of stars.

Orpheus (OR-fee-us): A musician, a poet, and a real charmer.

Pandora (pan-DOR-ah): The first human woman. Accidentally opened a jar full of evil.

Prometheus (pruh-MEE-thee-us): Gave fire to mankind and was sentenced to eternal torture by bird-pecking.

Satyrs (SAY-ters): 50 percent goat, 50 percent human. 100 percent party animal.

Silenus (sy-LEE-nus): Dionysus's best friend. Old and wise, but not that good at beast-care.

Tritons (TRY-tunz): Fish-tailed guards with human torsos. Probably also have fish brains.

PLACES

Arcadia (ar-CAY-dee-a): Wooded hills in Greece where the nymphs like to play.

Macris (mahk-REES): Big island off mainland Greece, shaped like a sea horse. Where Poseidon has his above-water palace.

Styx (STICKS): A dark river separating the Underworld from the land of the living.

Tartarus (TAR-ta-russ): A delightful torture dungeon miles below the Underworld.

BEASTS

Abraxas (uh-BRAK-suss): One of Helios's immortal horses, destined to pull the sun across the sky forever.

Basilisk (BASS-uh-lisk): King of the serpents. Every bit of him is pointy, poisonous, or perilous.

Centaur (SEN-tor): Half man, half horse, and lucky enough to get the best parts of both.

Cerberus (SUR-ber-uss): Three-headed guard dog whose only weaknesses are sunshine and happiness.

Cretan Bull (KREE-tun): A furious, fire-breathing bull. Don't stand too close.

Griffin (GRIH-fin): Couldn't decide if it was better to be a lion or an eagle, so decided to be both.

Hippocamp (HIP-oh-camp): Beast with a horse's head and a fishy tail. Like a sea horse, but bigger, scalier, and dumber.

Hydra (HY-druh): Nine-headed water serpent. Hera somehow finds this lovable.

Ladon (LAY-dun): A many-headed dragon that never sleeps (maybe the heads take turns?).

Manticore (MAN-tik-or): A spiky, hairy, hungry, lion-like, man-eating monster with a tail like a scorpion or snake.

Minotaur (MIN-uh-tor): A monster-man with the head of a bull. Likes eating people.

Nemean Lion (NEE-mee-un): A giant, indestructible lion. Swords and arrows bounce off his fur.

Stymphalian Birds (stim-FAY-lee-un): Man-eating birds with metal feathers, metal beaks, and toxic dung.

ABOUT THE AUTHOR

Lucy Coats studied English and ancient history at Edinburgh University, then worked in children's publishing, and now writes full-time. She is a gifted children's poet and writes for all ages from two to teenage. She is widely respected for her lively retellings of myths. Her twelve-book series Greek Beasts and Heroes was published by Orion in the UK. Beasts of Olympus is her first US chapter-book series. Lucy's website is at www.lucycoats.com. You can also follow her on Twitter @lucycoats.

ABOUT THE ILLUSTRATOR

As a kid, **Brett Bean** made stuff up to get out of trouble. As an adult, Brett makes stuff up to make people happy. Brett creates art for film, TV, games, books, and toys. He works on his tan and artwork in California with his wife, Julie Anne, and son, Finnegan Hobbes. He hopes to leave the world a little bit better for having him. You can find more about him and his artwork at www.2dbean.com.

ALSO AVAILABLE